Touched

Touched

Linda Armstrong-Miller

Writers Club Press
San Jose New York Lincoln Shanghai

Touched

All Rights Reserved © 2000 by Linda Armstrong-Miller

No part of this book may be reproduced or transmitted in any form or by any means, graphic, electronic, or mechanical, including photocopying, recording, taping, or by any information storage retrieval system, without the permission in writing from the publisher.

Writers Club Press
an imprint of iUniverse.com, Inc.

For information address:
iUniverse.com, Inc.
620 North 48th Street, Suite 201
Lincoln, NE 68504-3467
www.iuniverse.com

ISBN: 0-595-13918-3

Printed in the United States of America

Part I

Seven o'clock. Just two hours since my first night of call began. Only two hours but it felt more like two days. In that two hours, I've received absolutely no calls of any kind. Zero! I haven't even received a wrong page. I'm not complaining but if I'm going to be doing nothing I'd rather be doing nothing at home.

Instead, I was sitting in a strange room, on a strange bed, watching a baseball game on a strange TV, which by the way has such poor reception that there is almost no reception at all. All in all things could be worse. I suppose. Lord knows I was told how bad things could get at least a hundred times each day for the last few days.

I guess I could consider myself lucky that nothing has happened yet, bad or otherwise. I was sure that wouldn't hold out for long. Being lucky isn't something I've experienced a lot of over the years. Proof of that was my presence in this intern program.

Five days ago, I took one step closer to becoming a doctor. More to the point, I became an intern. Now here I sat wanting to be anywhere but here. It's bad enough I settled for a program I didn't want to be in. My reasons for doing that are strictly personal and had those reasons not been so personal I would have walked out already.

What makes things doubly bad for me is that this program has slots for six interns but only four of those positions are filled. That by itself isn't the problem. The fact that they lied to me is.

For now, I sit watching a baseball game and trying to decide where to go from here. I fluffed my pillows then settled back to watch as the pitcher quickly digs himself into a three and one hole. Just as he got a full count my beeper went off.

The number displayed on my beeper belonged to the ICU. The Intensive Care Unit and the Cardiac Care Unit are the areas I'm responsible for tonight. However, if need be, I could receive patients from the ER, the floors or any other place a patient may became unstable.

"This is Dr. Green. I was paged."

"Dr. Green hi. This is Sadie Poole. Your transfer is here."

"Transfer?" I asked. My heart skipped a beat at the word. I sat up knowing this meant trouble. I looked up just as Luck walked out the door. She didn't bother to look back or wave good bye.

"What transfer Mrs. Poole? I wasn't told anything about a transfer and I don't know anything about a transfer. Who accepted this patient?"

The calmness in my voice belied what I was truly feeling. The speed of my questions did not. I fired my questions off so fast Sadie Poole was not able to answer them. That was okay with me. I didn't really expect an answer.

"Dr Charlesdale accepted the patient."

"Dr Charlesdale?" Sirens went off in my head as I checked off yet another lie. Dr Charlesdale had been present for report. Neither he nor Jean Woods informed me that they'd accepted a transfer. "Are there any initial orders?"

"Just to call you Dr Green."

"Thanks." I said hanging up.

I looked up just in time to see the pitcher walking off the mound with his head down. He too had been betrayed. At least his betrayal was due to his arm. Mine was by a team who claimed they wanted and needed me. His betrayal cost him a grand slam. Even if it cost him the game, he'll get over it. My betrayal went much deeper than that and I was not going to be so lucky as to get over it.

I flipped through my notebook for a list of numbers that I should have and in fact, was told to memorize by now. I hadn't bothered to memorize any numbers at this hospital because I hadn't liked being ordered to do such a ridiculous thing. I rebelled either because I was sure I knew my stuff and I wouldn't be using those numbers much or because I knew I wouldn't be staying long so I didn't bother wasting my time. I wasn't sure which.

I knew calling Jean Woods was forbidden but I didn't care. I knew questioning him was a no-no. However, I was going to do just that. If I wasn't satisfied with his answers, I would call Dr Charlesdale, attending and leader of this piece of crap program and I would keep calling until I was satisfied.

Before making my call, I wanted to make sure I hadn't missed anything. I went over everything Jean Woods said to me before he left. It was a rather long speech but none of his speech involved informing me of a transfer. That I was sure of.

"Mat." He'd said. "You're on your own. Don't call me until you have exhausted every avenue. Oh and be careful what you order. One wrong order and you could seriously injure or even kill someone."

"Do yourself a big favor. Please listen to the nurses. They'll cover your ass if you don't piss them off. Most will tell you indirectly. If you don't listen then expect them to be very direct. At which point, they'll call me and of course that means I'll have to notify Dr Charlesdale at rounds.

"Oh and please don't write stupid orders. If you do, you'll never live it down. A fate that won't kill you but you represent all of us. If they're laughing at you, they're laughing at all of us." Jean went on and on like that until I shut him out.

This transfer had surprised me. I didn't like surprises and I thought Jean Woods should know that. Especially since it was Jean, himself, that told me his worst experience his first night of call had been getting an unexpected transfer.

Jean's story was only one of the many I heard about over the last five days. Everyone thought I would be better prepared if I knew about some of the things that could happen while on call. Their stories had just the opposite effect. Instead of preparing me, they simply stroked my imagination, which increased my fear.

I dialed Jean's house. He answered on the third ring.

"Hello."

"May I speak with Dr Woods please?"

"This is he." He said then took a deep breath. "Mat is that you?"

"Yes it is."

"Is everything all right?"

His question came much too quick. So quick, in fact, that he cut me off before I could state my reason for calling. There was no doubt in my mind. He already knew why I was calling.

"Listen Jean did you accept a transfer?" I asked not letting myself be side tracked by his theatrics.

"Yeah. I told you about her. Remember?"

"No Jean I do not remember. I've got the report you handed me right here. There is no mention of a transfer."

"Oh. Well that was my mistake Mat. I got the call at the last minute. I discussed it with Dr Charlesdale and I could have sworn I told you. I just forgot. Is she there?"

"Yes."

"How is she?"

"I don't know. I wanted to make sure she was ours before going to see her."

"She's ours. Let me think." He said and that made me want to reach through the phone and grab him by the throat. He wasn't very good at lying. I guess he was so good at everything else he didn't realize that.

"She's a ninety-eight year old black female who suffered from a heat stroke. Some kids found her in an abandon house yesterday. I think she also has a history of congestive heart failure and um…that's all I can recall at the moment. I just remember Dr. Charlesdale wanting to bring her in to work her up."

"Why bring her into the unit to work her up?"

"Are you swamped Mat? You need me to come in?" He asked challenging me.

"No. I don't need you to come in. I just wanted to know what was going on. That's all."

"Okay. Is there anything else?"

"No." I said then hung up the phone. "Just who in the hell does he think he's dealing with." I asked my empty room.

I was more than a little miffed at him, Dr Charlesdale and this program. I knew what they were doing. He didn't forget to tell me about this transfer. He was using it for an excuse. He hoped it would give him a reason to come in without looking like he was checking up on me.

"Well you won't be getting that reason from me. Not tonight."

Jean Woods didn't ever forget. Not ever. His reputation was built on always being prepared. It was known hospital wide that he never got a question wrong or a diagnosis for that matter. He was always right and I hated him for that. I threw my pillow across the room then stood.

"Okay Mat they want you to fail. So don't." I told myself.

I grabbed my jacket and put it on. I grabbed my stethoscope and swung it over my shoulder. When I was as psyched about going to the unit as I was going to get, I opened the door and stepped into the hallway.

I entered the ICU trying to look more relaxed than I really was. It didn't take me long to realized I didn't have to pretend. My entry went unnoticed. Every nurse was busy inside room six. Since everyone was in there, I decided to stay out.

I went to sit at the nurse's station. Standing in front of it, I realized I'd been wrong. Not everyone was in room six.

"You must be Dr Green. Hi, I'm Sadie Poole. All her paper work is on the table. I haven't had time to look at it yet."

"What do you know about her?"

"Just that she's ninety-eight years old and has a bad heart. She told me she knows for sure that she has congestive heart failure but that she also thought she had sick sinus syndrome. But she told me her real problem is simply that she's old." Sadie said then laughed. "She's a real sweet heart. She likes to be called Grandma by the way. The name on her record is Ruthie Mae Morris though."

"Did you know she was coming?"

"Yeah." She said looking at me.

Her tone of voice said 'of course I knew. That's how things are supposed to be done and so they are.' I envied her. In nursing, rules were more concrete.

I watched as Sadie Poole programmed Ruthie Mae Morris' name into the telemetry monitor. By doing this, it allowed other nurses to monitor Mrs. Morris' heart rhythm and rate, as well as any other patient's rhythm and rate, from the nurse's station. It kept all the nurses informed on all patients in case someone had to leave the floor for whatever the reason may be.

Once that task was completed, Sadie Poole went into the clean utility room to gather things such as a bedpan, IV tubing and the likes. When she was done there, she went into the linen closet. When she came out, her arms were loaded with blankets and pillows on top of all the other items she had gathered. When she stepped in to room six, she had everything she needed to care and provide comfort for Mrs. Morris.

Mrs. Morris, a patient who at this point, had no reason to be in the ICU. I should have followed Sadie Poole into room six. That would have given me the perfect opportunity to see the patient for myself. Instead, I sat down at the nurse's station.

I didn't want to be here. I didn't want to spend the rest of my life taking care of non-compliant patient with diabetes and high blood pressure. Patients who eventually went into renal failure or congestive heart failure. I didn't have the patience to take care of patients who didn't take care of themselves. But here I was.

I looked at the monitor. Ruthie Mae Morris' assessment of herself was probably the most accurate. She was old. Nothing I could do for her was going to change that. With that knowledge, she should have been sent anywhere but to a unit.

On the monitor, I saw an irregular rhythm. It was atrial fib. I wasn't concerned or impressed by that rhythm. Older people develop this rhythm and live without any problems. I looked from the monitor to room six. A whole entourage of nurses was spilling out. It was now my turn to go in.

Just as I started to stand, the alarms on the monitor went off and I turned back to see paper being spit from the printer. I pressed the stop button then looked at what had triggered the alarm. It was easy enough. Mrs. Morris heart rate had been seventy-four then it was one hundred and forty-four now it was thirty-four. That just about sums up sick sinus syndrome.

"Good Lord." I moaned, wondering not for the first time why I'd gone into medicine. Before I started the long drawn out process of convincing myself why I'd gone into medicine yet again, Sadie Poole walked up and interrupted me.

"Dr Green what labs do you want ordered? Grandma had an IV but it's no good now. I can get your labs while I'm starting her IV."

"How's she doing?"

"Fine. She's not complaining of any chest pain. She does have a headache but that's probably due to the nitro drip she has hanging. She's not one to complain though. I was doing a head to toe assessment and I had to practically drag that information out of her." Sadie Poole said. Her whole face lit up when she spoke of her patient. "That lady is so full of life. I hope I can be that sharp when I'm her age."

"That's all well and good Mrs. Poole but that hardly qualifies her for this unit." Sadie stared at me for a moment.

"Who pissed in your corn flakes doctor? You admitted her. If you didn't think she should have been here, you shouldn't have sent her here."

"I didn't." I told her but she had already turned to leave.

"I'm going to draw blood and leave it in the room. I don't want to have to stick her twice. If you order something, I'll send them off. If you don't, no harm done."

When her back was turned to me, she made a gesture at two of her co-workers. I couldn't see what that gesture was but it caused them to look at me.

"Mrs. Poole what's her code status?"

"Full code."

"Get a full panel then. I need to see what her electrolytes are."

If she heard my order, she didn't acknowledge it. She was walking away when I spoke and she continued to walk away without pausing or even glancing back. I looked at her two co-workers. They were still looking at me.

I'd just made a fatal mistake. Without actually saying the words, I told these nurses I didn't want to take care of that patient and they didn't like it. In the short time she'd been here, she'd made some strong allies. In just as short a time, I'd made some strong enemies.

Jean Woods had warned me. I now remembered a portion of his speech that I'd only halfway listened to.

"The nurses in the unit are dedicated to their patient. Their sole goal is to take care of them. Sometimes that care doesn't always involve medicine but a touch, a kind word to the patient. If not the patient then the family. For the family, they also lend an attentive ear and a gentle touch. I realized that the nurses' goals and my goals were not the same.

From this night on, I knew they would cut me no slack. They will not hesitate to go up the chain just so they don't have to deal with me. They will never trust me and therefore double check and triple check all my orders. By tomorrow morning, Jean Woods will know how they feel about me and so will Dr Charlesdale.

Tonight was the beginning of a long four years. I sat back and thought about something I could fix. Congestive heart failure I could fix.

Congestive heart failure is a condition in which fluid backs up into the lungs. This happens because the heart, which is a pump, isn't pumping effectively. In order to change this, I must improve the pump. Digoxin is the drug of choice for that.

Once the lungs get loaded with fluids, a patient starts experiencing difficulty breathing. If gone untreated, the patient can literally drown. I can fix that too. Lasix is the drug of choice for that.

Sick sinus syndrome is another story all together. The bottom line is this condition will ultimately require a pacemaker. At ninety-eight, putting a pacemaker in her would be a waste of time. At the most, it may buy her another year. Age alone has the upper hand here.

She's ninety-eight years old for crying out loud! By her own admission, her biggest problem is she's too old. Yet she's a full code. This lady had the potential to be a major pain in my backside, I thought sitting down at the table outside of her room and opening her chart.

The first thing I looked for in her chart was the transfer summary. It would give me a better idea why she was here. There was no summary.

Okay, I thought, looking for her progress notes. I hoped there would be something there for me to work with. The only progress note on her chart told me that she had an eighteen gauge IV and that she had complained of chest pain. It didn't even tell me what time her nitro drip was started or how fast.

I looked for her history. There wasn't one. How was that possible? Based on what I was looking at, this patient's only documented treatment was an IV.

Nothing else was done for this patient. Not a thing. According to the law, if it's not documented it wasn't done. There wasn't even a note telling me this patient consented to being transferred.

"Great! She's a dump!" I muttered.

I wanted to be surprised but I wasn't. As far as I was concerned, she was a dump for me twice over. Once by Jean Woods and Dr Charlesdale because they failed to tell me about her. The second time by the facility that transferred her.

I wrote orders for medications I knew I would be giving her. I knew she was on a nitro drip because Sadie Poole had told me as much, so I wrote to continue that. I ordered lab work for the blood that Sadie Poole had already drawn then I was stumped. I could go no farther without going in and assessing the patient.

Since there wasn't a history already on the chart, I needed to write a history. In order to write that history, I needed to find out what else may be wrong with her. I needed to find out why she was in an abandoned house. All of these things would have to be answered before morning rounds. But they didn't have to be answered right now.

"Oh what the hell Mat! Get it over with." I muttered to myself.

I took a deep breath and stood. I looked for Sadie Poole. I would need her for a few minutes while I examined the patient. To my surprise, I was alone. Here was the prefect opportunity to leave. If anyone asked, I could always say I was called away.

Before turning to leave, something told me to look into Mrs. Morris' room. As soon as I did, I wished I hadn't. There, staring out at me were the most alert, clear and very much alive eyes I've every seen on a person of ninety-eight or any other age for that matter.

Those eyes were luminous and sort of eerie yet they some how conveyed a warmth that I couldn't explain. I'd already declared this woman not long of this world. For someone with that sentence, those eyes exhumed nothing but life. I looked into those eyes then looked away. In the darkened room, her eyes were all I could see of her.

Out of the corner of my eye, I saw movement. My window of escape had slowly slipped away. With no other option and now an audience of nurses once again, I stepped inside Mrs. Morris' room. I didn't look at her right away. Nor did I speak to her.

Initially, I only stepped into the doorway. Now I took another step into the room. There was no doubt in my mind that I was capable of caring for this patient. What was bothering me was why should I?

I looked back and realized there was still too much activity for me to just leave. Questions would be asked. Questions I didn't mind answering tonight but questions I didn't want to deal with in the morning.

I looked at Mrs. Morris. What I'd observed while standing in the hallway was nothing compared to what I was faced with now. Those large luminous eyes were not just all I could see of her. They were all there was of her. Then just as quickly, I was faced with a little old black lady, a whole little old lady lying in bed. Not just a pair of eyes.

I stood with one foot in front of the other ready to back out. Everything in my being told me to get the hell out. I didn't. Instead, I fought hard to stay put. It had to have been and illusion. I hoped that's all it had been. It had looked real. Whatever it was, it wasn't now. So I stayed.

"Hello Mrs. Morris how are you doing?" I asked and realized my voice was trembling. I took a deep breath and tried to calm down.

"Alive Matthew Allen. Much to your dissatisfaction." She said.

"Excuse me?" I asked actually, totally thrown by her answer. Her answer was not an illusion. I'd heard her right and her answer had shocked me.

So shocked, in fact, that I did take a step backward. In doing so, I realized I felt a fear that I could not rationalize. As if her answer wasn't bad enough, she'd called me by my first and middle name. This was a woman I have never met yet she knew something about me that she should not have known.

"Mrs. Morris?" I asked.

She didn't answer me. She just laid quietly in that darken room with her eyes closed. She acted as if nothing out of the ordinary had just happened. It had though. Twice! I looked at the monitor. A blue line reading respiratory indicated that she was breathing at thirteen reps a minute.

Her heart rate was seventy-four. But from where I stood she looked as if she had died. Her body was motionless.

I took a step closer. When she didn't move, I took one more tentative step in her direction. I felt like a mouse approaching cheese on a loaded mousetrap. I felt the trap would snap close around my head and neck at any minute. And it did!

"Matthew Allen do you believe two wrongs make a right?" She asked.

Her question was so unexpected that it scared me. My heart skipped a beat and I realized that I was holding my breath. I was afraid. This realization angered me.

"Mrs. Morris what in the hell are you talking about?" I asked much to loud.

Her question had made no sense under the current circumstance. But then neither did my outburst. My face flushed as it slowly dawned on me that I was over reacting to a simple question and a frail old black lady. To make matters worse, my outburst brought Sadie Poole running.

"Is everything all right?" She asked looking at me then at Mrs. Morris. Mrs. Morris laid quietly pretending to be asleep.

"Mrs. Poole where are the transfer papers and the other paperwork that came with this patent?" I asked not really sure why I'd chosen that defense but glad that I had.

Sadie Poole immediately backed out of the room and opened Mrs. Morris' chart. She flipped through the chart much as I had. When she came up empty, she came back into the room where I'd stayed.

"I'll call the hospital that she came from and I'll get in touch with the ambulance that transported her. I should be able to locate them or get copies of them." She stated very matter of fact but with just a small amount of uncertainty.

"Thank you. Before you go, will you stick around so that I can examine Mrs. Morris?"

"Sure thing!" She said more than happy to stay and help take care of this patient. A patient that I still couldn't justify having in my care at this very moment, nor did I want.

"Grandma how's that headache?" Sadie Poole asked before I could speak.

"All but gone child. Now you stop fretting over me so. I'm just fine."

"This is Dr Green. He wants to examine you."

"That's just fine with me." She said. "The two of us have already made acquaintance."

I started to speak but didn't. I never introduced myself to her. What was she talking about? Further more, what was she up to?

Unsure where to start or what to say, I pulled my index cards from my pocket. On those cards, I had a running log of all the patients that were under my care at the moment. I started one on Mrs. Morris.

This gave me something to do without drawing questions or suspicion from Sadie Poole. After a moment, I was literally saved by the bell. The phone rang. When no one picked it up after the fourth ring, Sadie Poole excused herself, leaving me alone with a woman that I found to be totally spooky.

I kept my head down while Sadie Poole was gone. I wasn't really writing anything because there was nothing to write. I hadn't examined the patient. It simply gave me a reason not to speak to the patient.

"Is there a problem Matthew Allen?" She asked as soon as Sadie Poole was gone.

"Should there be?" I asked looking up at her.

Again I wished I hadn't. Confronting me were those large, eerie, luminous eyes. This was no trick. From where I was standing, which was at the foot of her bed, I saw nothing but eyes. Mrs. Morris was gone! I placed my hand over my mouth to stifle a scream.

Those eyes had replaced the woman that had only a few moments ago lay in that bed. I dropped the cards I'd been writing my notes on and backed up until my back was against the wall. I blew air into my hands. It was meant to be a scream but all that came out was forced air.

I needed to get out of this room, out of this unit, away from this woman. But I didn't move. I couldn't move. And it was probably a good thing I couldn't. For if I could have moved at this particular moment, I would have went running and screaming from the room like I'd lost my mind.

"Matthew Allen does two wrongs make a right?" I heard.

I heard this but I wasn't sure how I'd heard it. She shouldn't have been capable of speech. She had no mouth. She had no nose. She had no face. She had only eyes. Large luminous eyes.

I stood staring, my own eyes wide with shock and fear. Then just like that the eyes were gone. In their place was that frail ninety-eight year old black lady. I heard Sadie Poole before I saw her. Thank God!

When she walked into the room, I was on one knee picking up my cards.

"Okay Dr. Green sorry about that."

"No problem." I muttered from the floor. "I have to go anyway. I was just paged. I'll be back as soon as I can." I said standing and leaving as fast as I could.

Once outside the unit, I stood with my red-hot face pressed against a cold cinder block that made up the walls. I couldn't shake the feeling that I was being watched. So strong was the feeling, that I was sure if I closed my eyes, I would see those disembodied eyes watching me. So sure was I, that I didn't close my eyes.

I looked in both directions to see if I was alone. When I realized that I was, I placed my back against the wall and tried to clear my head. That very act reminded me of my back being against the wall in Mrs. Morris' room. I looked ahead of me expecting to see those haunting eyes.

Instead, I saw a block wall identical to the one my back was against. I took a deep breath. I was shaking all over. Both physically and mentally.

Who was she? How did she know me? How was she able to make herself disappear? All but her eyes that is. But most importantly what did she want with me.

Sweat dripped from my temples. My throat was having a difficult time doing what my brain was ordering it to do. That's because my brain was having a hard time giving out orders. Every time I tried to comprehend what had happened, I simply lost the ability to think. It was like thoughts were reaching for the door of my brain only to find that the door was locked.

"Okay Mat." I said out loud. "What happened in there?"

I paced back and forth no longer able to stand still. I hoped that speaking would make processing possible.

"Okay." I said. "First you were bored out of your mind. Then you got a surprise patient. That patient of course does not require your care but she's here.

"Once here, you find out that she was a dump. She knew who you were before you introduced yourself. She asked you a stupid question and you went off the deep end.

"No. No. First she did that thing with her eyes then she asked the stupid question. Then she did the eye thing again."

I stopped talking but kept pacing. Nothing I said was making sense anyway. Recapping the events that led to me pacing in the hall and talking to myself only made matters worse. Besides, whatever the events, they all came down to one thing. That old black woman scared the hell out of me.

What had she said to me anyway? "Fine Matthew Allen much to your dissatisfaction." What had she meant by that? Had she known what I was thinking?

"No! No way Mat!" I said scolding myself.

I needed to get a grip. There was an explanation for what had happened. I just needed to figure out what it was.

"But losing control wasn't going to help." I reminded myself.

She knew I didn't want her here. No amount of rationalization was going to prove otherwise.

"Think Mat. How had she known that?"

She could have gotten that from my actions. I did ask Sadie Poole what her code status was. Maybe she heard me? Then I sat outside of her room flipping angrily through her chart.

"See Mat. There's your answer." I said.

That made me feel better but no matter how long I thought about it, I could not explain how she knew me or how she'd made…It was an illusion. That's what it was! I wanted to believe that so bad I ruled out everything else.

I knew one thing. I had to find out. I was not going to spend the rest of my night quivering in my boots. I placed both my hands on the doors to the unit. My intention was to confront my fears.

Where did that thought come from? I haven't had thoughts along those lines since my father died. I can remember him saying, "Matthew, son, confront whatever you're feeling. If after you have done that and you still don't like something, you don't have to do it. But don't write something off because it scares you."

I stood with both hands on those doors but I didn't push. Tears stung my eyes. I haven't thought about my father in a long time. He died when I was only eight and nothings been the same since.

"Well no time for reminiscing now." I said pushing the doors.

I needed to go back into the unit. I was going to march into room six and right up to that old lady's bed and demand an answer. At least, that was my intention. Instead, my beeper went off.

I weighted my options. If I went into the unit to answer the page, eyebrows would be raised. I would also have to put off for a second time Mrs. Morris' exam. The best thing for me to do would be to answer this page in the call room.

Walking to the call room seemed to calm me. Maybe it wasn't the walk. Maybe it was the knowledge that I had a legitimate reason not to take that march into room six. Whatever was responsible, I was thankful. That state of confusion had worn me down.

Once inside the call room, I washed my face. When my beeper went off a second time, I realized that I needed to get my rear in gear. Both of the pages had come from the same number. Great!

"This had better be and emergency." I said watching my trembling hand dial the displayed number.

"Lakeland ER. This is Ms Pitchers. May I help you?"

"This is Dr. Green. I was paged." I said.

"Hold one moment Dr. Green. Dr. White paged you in reference to a code we have coming in."

"Okay." I was placed on hold for about ten seconds then another female voice answered the phone.

"Dr. Green this is Dr. White. I have a sixty-eight year old white male down here that was just brought in. The family told the EMT's that his wife found him.

"A neighbor was called and he initiated CPR. We've got a blood pressure of sixty over thirty-five. Patient is intubated. I need you to come admit him." She finished.

Admit what? I thought but didn't say. Sixty over thirty-five wouldn't support life.

"How long has he been down now Dr. White?"

"No one knows."

"Okay." I said and was hung up on.

That alone burned my buns but it was far from the only thing. Now wasn't the time to dwell on it so I grabbed my things and ran for the stairs.

I took the stairs down two at a time and came out on the first floor. The exercise alone did what talking out loud had not been able to do. It unlocked my brain.

As I ran down the hall that led to the ER, it crossed my mind that if we used enough vasopressors, we could clamp his vascular system down enough to improve his blood pressure. I could admit him into the unit and let Jean Woods and Dr Charlesdale deal with the rest of his care and his family tomorrow.

I entered the ER running. A crowd was located outside of room two. I walked in, took one look at the patient then looked around for Dr White. How dare she waste my time?

No amount of vasopressors was going to help this man. Even if we used a pacemaker on him, it would probably not save his life. Still, I approached him trying not to let what I felt show.

"Stop compressions." I said.

I listened. There was no heartbeat. The was no spontaneous breathing once artificial breathing was suspended. In fact, the patient was mottled.

His whole chest, neck and both arms down to his elbow had purple splotches on them. On top of all that, his lips were blue. Even with him being intubated and receiving one hundred percent oxygen, he still was not alive enough to use that oxygen.

"Are we sure this tube is in the right place?" I asked.

"It is according to the x-ray." I was told.

That did it! There was nothing I could do for this man. Why had I been called? I was just an intern. Surely an ER attending didn't need me to confirm that this man was dead.

"Continue CPR." I said.

I turned to Dr White. No amount of medication, compressions, oxygen or electricity was going to bring back the dead.

"Dr White?" I asked extending my hand. "Did you get a better idea of how long he's been down?"

"Yes. We're looking at about thirty-five minutes."

I narrowed my eyes and made the second mistake of the night. I chuckled. I knew right away it had been a mistake and I also knew right away that she did not like it or me.

"Is there something funny Dr Green?" Her voice was cold and hard?

"No I suppose there isn't." I said.

What I was really thinking was yeah, you. For all intents and purposes, my spoken answer was the better of the two.

"Stick around." She ordered. Her countenance softened some but not enough to let me off the hook.

"It doesn't look like you'll be needing me Dr. White." I said getting ready to protest the misuse of my time. Instead, her hard, cold stare stopped me. "Fine, I'll be around." I said then turned my back to her.

I found a wall and propped against it, much as I'd done outside of the unit. I was in full view of the patient and the attendant. I looked her way once. Once was more than enough.

She was still staring at me. And she was madder than a queen bee. On more than one occasion, she let her eyes travel from my head to my feet then back up. It was like she was memorizing everything about me.

When I thought I was no longer the focus of her attention, she let her eyes start at my head then traveled back down to my feet again. A silly childhood saying popped into my mind. It took everything I had not to say, 'Why don't you take a picture. It'll last longer.'

I had to press my lips firmly together to keep from laughing. Despite my efforts, I think she still suspected that I was laughing at her. As if she couldn't believe my attitude, she threw one hand up, palm facing me then walked off.

Well Matty old boy, you'll pay for that. Matty? I haven't referred to myself as Matty in years. No one else had either. I shook my head to clear it. Why was I having all these weird thoughts from the past?

I looked in at the patient. Nothing had changed so I thought about all the damage I'd done tonight. I was willing to think of anything to forget my childhood memories including my upcoming ER rotation.

Three months, I thought, and you'll be all hers Mat. She's going to make your life miserable. Just you wait and see.

I felt reasonably sure I could appease her if I called the unit and told them we had a patient. But I refused to do that. If she wanted a boost of confidence, she wasn't going to get it from me. I knew what she really wanted. She wanted to keep her stats up while bringing mine down.

Well not tonight lady. I saw no need in transferring a dead body to the unit only to have to declare it dead then transfer it to the morgue. If she wanted to play games then we would. Time was on my side.

She went to the phone. While looking at me, she picked it up and dialed. I stayed put against that wall. She was playing chicken and I refuse to flinch. Fifteen minutes later, she called the code and pronounced the patient dead.

I wrote a quick summary then left the ER with my right arm crossed over my body. This position kept me from throwing my chest out and strutting. I'd won the battle but the war would begin in three months.

I rode an empty elevator back to the third floor. Once there, I decided to finish what I'd started. Again, I walked back to the unit. I placed both hands on those doors with the intention of pushing them open, going into room six, marching up to that old bag of bones and demanding what was going on.

Instead, I jerked both hands away as soon as I placed them on the doors. It felt like my left hand had been placed on a hot stove. The right hand felt as if it'd been pressed against the side of a freezer's wall. Both were hurting.

My left hand had blisters forming over the entire surface. It burned and stung something awful. I looked at my right hand. The surface was missing the entire layer of skin. It also was burning and stinging.

I stood in the hall outside the unit blowing and shaking both hands. Without warning, I got the unmistakable feeling I was being watched. I looked at those unit doors, which should have been made of solid wood. They weren't. In the center were Grandma's large, luminous eyes.

I did what I'd wanted to do earlier. I ran! In the heat of the moment, I forgot about my damaged hands. I simply balled both fist and ran.

I didn't have far to go. The call room was on the same floor. It was only three doors down and around the corner. I raced around that corner doing top speed and hit the door to the call room so hard I literally bounced backwards.

Stupid thoughts never cease to amaze me. They're liable to pop up anywhere. Like the stupid thoughts I'd had in the ER and the one that I was having now.

When I bounced off that wall, I thought of cartoons. In my mind's eye, I saw myself as a cartoon. I was Bluto. Popeye had just hit me. The door was a cartoon block wall and that was why I'd bounced off it.

This all would have been funny had it not been so pathetic. I reached into my pants pocket and located the key. It was at that point that I realized my hands were no longer hurting. Upon inspection, I found my hands were no longer damaged. I found no burns, blisters or missing skin.

I stared at my left hand while I unlocked the door with my right. They were normal. What was wrong with me? Had I snapped?

I stepped into the call room's bathroom. I looked at my face. I looked into my eyes. I looked the same.

I saw nothing out of the ordinary. If I was crazy I couldn't see it. I looked at my hands again. Normal. I looked normal. So if I was going crazy how would anyone know? As a crazy man, would I do something dangerous?

"No Mat." I said. "You'll just see things that aren't there." After a short pause, I added. "And talk to yourself."

I stepped from the bathroom into the main part of the call room. It was really nothing more than an old patient's room that was no longer used. It's only difference was that it was equipped with a computer.

I looked around. I didn't feel watched but I looked for those disembodied eyes anyway. When I was satisfied I was alone, I took a deep breath in an attempt to relax.

Slowly I took my lab jacket off. I threw it across the back of the room's only chair. Then I kicked both shoes off. One slid under the bed while the other went straight up in the air. I had to duck to keep from getting hit by my own shoe.

That did it! I started giggling. From giggling, I gave way to a full fledge laugh. I lay on the bed half dressed trying to stop. When I couldn't, I knew that I had indeed snapped. That image and that thought made me laugh that much harder.

After countless minutes of laughing, I looked at my watch. To make sure I was seeing correctly I looked at the clock on the nightstand. It was twelve thirty. Realizing that five and a half-hours had passed by sobered me in a way nothing else had. I've had a patient in the unit for five and a half hours without an examination or an assessment.

I reached for the phone and dialed the unit.

"ICU Mrs. Robins may I help you?"
"Mrs. Robins, this is Dr Green. May I speak with Sadie Poole?"
"Hold."

While I held, I took my pants and shirt off. Now I knew I was crazy. I was undressed except for my shorts. If a code were called now, I'd never make it. Rule number one for being on call, I was told, was not to undress.

"As soon as you do Mat, they'll call a code ninety-nine. It never fails. Getting undressed or taking a dump." I was told.

"This is Sadie Poole."
"Mrs. Poole, this is Dr. Green. How is Mrs. Morris?"
"She's doing just fine. Jean is talking with her right now." That response caught me by surprise.
"Dr Woods is there?"
"Yeah, he just showed up. You want me to tell him to page you."

"Just tell him I'm back in the call room." I told her then hung up. "You couldn't stand it could you Jean? You just had to come in." I said to the empty call room.

Just what pushed you over the edge I wondered? Did Sadie Poole call you or did that obnoxious Dr White. Actually, I didn't give a damn which one called him. Before coming in, he should have called me and got my side of the story.

Since he didn't, to hell with him! It's twelve forty-five a.m. If he wants to spend his time checking up on me, he was more than welcomed to do so.

With that thought, I laid down and turned out the light. I laid on my back, with my hands laying at rest on my chest and I stared at the ceiling. I tried not to dwell on his being here but I couldn't help it. My reaction had changed from not giving a damn to being angry. This was my night.

I laid in the dark waiting. Sooner or later he would call me. Just like Dr White, Jean Woods was playing a game. It too was one that I could win. I had time on my side. I had to be here all night. If Jean didn't want to be here as long, he'll find me and square things away.

At one o'clock he called to do just that. "This is Dr. Green." I said trying not to sound irritated but hoping I did.

"Hello Mat. This is Jean." He said then was quiet. I was too. He called me. If he had something to say he could carry the conversation. "Mat are you still there?"

"Yeah Jean I'm here. Is it true you're here too?"

"Fraid so."

"Why?"

"It seems you pissed Dr White off. She called Dr. Charlesdale to report that you weren't very helpful with a patient she called you about."

"The man was dead Jean. What did she want me to do?"

"I agree with you Mat. I went over the code summary. I looked over your note and I told her I had to agree with your findings. That didn't make her feel a whole lot better but she did back down. The point was your attitude. She said you were rude. Any truth to that?"

"Absolutely not!" I said.

"You didn't laugh at her Mat?"

"I wanted to." I said.

"I see. Well I'll call Dr. Charlesdale and tell him Dr. White was just being Dr. White."

"You had to come all the way from home just to go over a code summary Jean?" I asked. The comment I really wanted to make was, 'stop jerking me around and tell me why you're here.'

"Not exactly." He said.

"Why exactly are you here Jean?"

"When I was trying to find you, I called the ICU. Sadie Poole answered. She told me you'd not assessed Mrs. Morris because you got called away."

"Why didn't you just page me?" He didn't answer right away.

I knew I was wearing his patience down but I wanted the truth. I wanted him to be man enough to own up to his actions.

"I assessed Mrs. Morris for you." He said instead. "I came in because I thought you were bogged down. I wrote some orders, a history that kind of stuff. Sadie will be calling you if anything's out of whack with her labs."

"You didn't have to do that Jean. I just called Mrs. Poole to let her know I was on my way back. There were enough orders to cover any circumstance until I could return. Image my surprise when she told me you were here."

"You feel I'm stepping on your toes Mat?"

"No Jean. I just want to know why you're checking up on me."

My voice was cool, calm but definitely accusatory. He was quiet for a long moment before he answered. He took a long deep breath then muttered something I couldn't hear.

"You want me to be honest with you Mat, so I will. You're not ready for call. Not by yourself anyway. I think we pushed you too fast and way too hard. Five days Mat. That's all the time we gave you. It wasn't long enough."

"I appreciate your honesty but I disagree. The best way to learn is to just get out there and do it. I would have called you long before I was in trouble. Dr. White's just upset because her stats took a hit tonight."

"So you don't need me?"

"No."

"Okay. I'm going to finish up here and I'm headed home. Good night."

"Good night." I said then hung up.

God I hated that man. Man hell! He wasn't a mere man. He was a god. I was competing with a god and as far as everyone was concern, I couldn't even hold a candle to him.

"Jean's talking with her now." Sadie Poole had said. She, like all the other nurses around here, loved him. As far as everyone was concerned, he could do no wrong. He looked good by making those around him look bad.

There was no need for him to talk with the ER attending. He should have spoken with me. There was no need for him to write my history or assess my patient. I could have done it.

Regardless of what I felt for that old lady, I knew what my job was and I would have done it. But by him doing it, it makes him look efficient, helpful, good. That was the bottom line. It made him look good.

And believe me Jean Woods always looked good. Why shouldn't he? He has it all. He's from a good family with good money and great connections. As if that wasn't enough, he looks a lot like the guy who plays the lead in The Mummy. I spend most days trying not to slip on the drool the nurses leave behind.

To hell with em! I'm just as good looking. On top of that, I've got dimples. The kind of dimples my mother assured me no woman would ever be able to resist. But I was more than a smile.

I graduated third in my class. I was smart god damn it! Not a soul around here knew it though.

To make matters worse, I'll have to walk in his shadow for at least another year. That's because he's destined to be the fellow next year. Hell, even Dr. Charlesdale liked Jean and that was no small accomplishment. Fine! All I wanted was to get through this night, this year and this program.

I rolled on to my side and thought about what had led me to become a doctor in the first place. As before, it didn't take me long to come to the strong conclusion that this was not what I wanted to be doing with my life, when my beeper went off. I looked at the clock before reaching for the phone. It was three forty-five. I couldn't believe it. I'd been asleep.

"This is Dr. Green. I was paged." I said still pleasantly surprised by the two-hour nap.

"Dr Green this is Sadie Poole." I heard and immediately my stomach lurched. "Grandma Morris' heart rate is in the low thirties. Atropine was given with no improvement. We've also titrated her nitro up. She was having more chest pain. But it's dropped her pressure."

"What's her pressure?"

"Ninety-eight over forty-two."

"Start a dopamine drip and get the trans…"

"Dr Green something's happening." Sadie Poole said interrupting me. "Her heart rate just increased to fifty-five."

"What's her pressure?"

"Hey Cindy re-cycle Grandma's cuff for me." We were both quiet while we waited. "One hundred and five over fifty-eight." She said.

"Let's sit on that. Start the dopamine anyway. Just in case her pressure drops. And next time Mrs. Poole, give the atropine time to work."

"Dr Green it's three fifty. We gave the atropine at three o'clock and three fifteen. Just how long would you recommend I wait? If I hadn't felt the need to call you, I wouldn't have." She said then the phone went dead.

Everything in my being told me to get up and go to the ICU. But the same rebellious streak that got me in trouble as a kid and most of my teen years told me not to and like then I listened. I turned the light out yet again.

When the phone didn't ring and my beeper didn't go off, I decided all was well. I placed my beeper on my chest, crossed my hands over it and fell back to sleep.

The high pitch noise started far away then moved closer to me. Closer still, until it was right in my face yelling. Yelling loud to 'wake up.' I opened my eyes and sat up. Immediately I felt disoriented. I closed my eyes and like a bat using radar I searched until I found the offensive noise, which was now lying on the bed beside me.

The room fell silent immediately. The disorientation, however, continued so I searched for a light source. Once the room was illuminated, the confusion past and I realized all was right with the world. I was just on call. Nothing more.

It was now four thirty. Once I realized the time, it made me see that all was not well with the world. All the world wasn't being awakened at four thirty in the morning. Just me.

I looked at my beeper and recognized the number as that of the ICU. I was receiving yet another call from none other than Sadie Poole about none other than Mrs. Morris. Jesus Christ!

Why was everyone making such a fuss over this old black lady? I wished she would just die. It would make everyone's life easier. Especially mine.

I wanted to ignore the page. Hell, to be honest, I wanted to turn the damned thing off. But if I did that, I'd have hell to pay when rounds met. Besides that, if I didn't answer, Sadie Poole would simply call Jean Woods. They would both love that.

"The old lady is dying!" I yelled into the empty room. "Dead actually. Am I the only one that can see the end is here?" I muttered shaking my head, dreading having to get up.

With no other choice that I could think of, I dialed the number to the unit. "What is it this time Mrs. Poole?" My mouth asked before my brain could stop it. As if she hadn't heard me and didn't care that I was irritated, she responded as cheery and as professional as I should have.

"Dr Green, Grandma Morris is complaining of shortness of breath. May I give her twenty milligrams of Lasix? She's got crackles in the bases of both lungs. Her blood pressure is one fourteen over fifty-two. Pulse ox ninety-three percent."

Just who's the doctor here? I wondered but didn't say. I remained quiet long enough to get her attention.

"Dr. Green are you there?"

"Why don't you give Mrs. Morris twenty milligrams of Lasix Mrs. Poole?" I said.

It was now her turn to get quiet. She would never understand what I was feeling. I've gone to school twice as long as she has, spent twice as much money on education than she ever will. I'm the one that has to put up with bullshit from bullshit attending not her. She wasn't the one I was angry with but she'd have to do.

I should have been happy she was on tonight. One day I will value her knowledge but not tonight.

"Anything else?"

"Yes. After we get her breathing better and of course if she's still requesting something, can she have something for a headache? The nitro we gave her made her headache worse. She's asking for Tylenol."

"Tylenol? A headache?" I asked for effect. "Why don't we deal with the important stuff first?" I said.

"Have it your way Dr Green. I was just trying to kill two birds with one stone. I'll give her twenty milligrams of Lasix. After that, if she's still complaining, I'll call you back. How's that?"

"Don't you dare!" I threaten then backed off.

"This is your patient. It's either call you or call Jean." It was her turn to threaten.

"That old lady is dying."

"The old lady that you are referring to is a full code. That entitles her to full care and that full care patient is complaining of a headache."

"Okay. Okay. I'll tell you what. Give her four milligrams of morphine IV every two hours as needed until her headache is relieved. That should make Mrs. Morris very comfortable."

"And send her right to the morgue." Sadie Poole said. That's where she's headed anyway. I thought but didn't say. "I'll do you one better Dr. Green." Sadie Poole said. "I'll draw the morphine up. You come on down and push it.

"In the meantime, I'll explain to the patient why you're trying to rush her out of this world. On second thought Dr Green, forget the Tylenol and the morphine and come on down anyway. Her heart rate just dropped to twenty-two." At that, the line was disconnected.

I dropped the phone in the cradle, cursed then dropped my head into my hands. "Damn it Mat! Do you always have to be such an asshole? All you had to do was agree to the orders."

There was nothing wrong with what Sadie Poole or the patient had requested. "You're gonna be up all night now. All you had to do was treat the patient. Now look what you've done." I said then stopped and looked around the empty room.

I was talking to myself again. Every time that old black lady was involved, I found myself talking to myself. I was dealing with all this grief because that old black lady refused to die.

I didn't care about her. I didn't even care about the man that died in the ER. Hell I didn't even like people!

Why hadn't I chosen a field that limited my contact with people? Live people anyway. I could have gone into research. There's plenty of money in research. It's not too late I thought looking at my watch.

Thirty seconds since Sadie Poole hung up on me. Time had taken on a whole new life tonight. Any other night, thirty seconds would have passed in the blink of an eye. Tonight, time was riding on the back of a snail.

Forty-five seconds after being hung up on, I looked under the bed for my shoe. One minute after Sadie Poole hung up on me, I'd located and was holding both shoes. I dropped them on the floor in front of me.

"Code 99 ICU! Code 99 ICU!"

"Fuck!" I yelled.

I pushed both feet into my shoes at the same time only to realize I didn't have my pants on. I stepped off my shoes and grabbed my pants. While I hopped around on one foot putting my pants on, I looked for my shirt. What had I done with that damn thing?

"Code 99 ICU! Code 99 ICU?" The voice barked over the intercom.

It had only been thirty seconds since the first call. The snail had died and a gazelle had taken its place. Time was now racing by me at a pace I couldn't keep up with.

I gave up looking for my shirt. I slipped my lab jacket on over my tee shirt, buttoned my pants and stepped back into my shoes. As I left the call room, the intercom clicked on again.

"Code 99 ICU! Code 99 ICU!"

Each time I heard that message, my brain played a nasty little trick on me. My ears heard the same message everyone else heard but my brain interpreted it to me as something else all together.

"Get you ass in gear Matthew Allen." My brain told me. "Get your ass in gear."

That was easier said than done. The harder I ran. The slower I moved. It didn't help that I didn't have my shoes on all the way. When I'd been forced to dress in a hurry, I'd flatten the heels of my shoes rather than take the time to untie and retie them. Now they made a flapflapflap sound as I ran.

Two minutes, thirty-seven seconds after Sadie Poole hung up on me, I entered the unit. Not very good time considering how close the unit was to the call room. Tomorrow the jokes would start, assuming I was still here tomorrow.

"Matthew Green is how not to be when responding to a code." Dr. Charlesdale will say with a straight face and a disapproving tone of voice.

The nicknames will also start. Names like turtle or snail or sprinter or the hundred-yard dash man. They will all be spoken with the same meaning. Matthew Green had responded to a code much too slow.

Four years. That's all I have to put up with any of it. I told myself as I approached the crowd that stood outside of room six.

Jean Woods was the last person I expected to see. In fact, I distinctly remembered him telling me good night, that he was going to finish up and head home. But there he was. He looked up and saw me approaching.

"Codes over Mat." He said looking at me then away and into room six.

"I thought you told me you were going home."

"Good thing I didn't. Don't you think?" He asked standing and taking me by the arm.

He led me away from room six and away from the crowd. When we were at the far end of the unit, he turned to face me.

"You look like shit Mat." He said frowning.

He took the time to size me up before speaking again. His glare reminded me of Dr. White's. The difference now was I had no crazy remarks running around in my head. I looked at myself then back at him. He was right but I said nothing.

We stared at each other for a moment. He shook his head then looked away.

"Sadie called you Mat. She didn't call me until you didn't show up. I was prepared to let you handle things. That is what you asked me to do. Isn't it?"

"Were you? Is that why there was a secret code between you and Mrs. Poole?"

"This isn't funny Dr. Green." He said. The use of Dr Green instead of Mat was his way of telling me he was no longer talking to me as a friend. Not that I ever considered him to be one. "You failed to respond to a code. No Mat it's worse than that. You failed to come when you were called."

"Is she all right?" I asked trying to defuse the situation. "I mean did she die?"

"Are you kidding?" He asked shaking his head.

Despite himself, he had to smile. I'd given him the illusion that I cared and that was something he could work with. He even relaxed a little.

"That old girl ain't going anywhere. Not just yet anyway. She's a gutsy old lady. I've got to give her that. She's made of some stern stuff."

He leaned against the wall and crossed his ankles. "We should all be so strong. Heck, she told me it wasn't her time to go yet." He allowed himself another smile. "Close though she said. She ought to know." He nodded his head then he laughed.

"Huh?" I asked narrowing my eyes and looking at him closer. Maybe I wasn't the one who'd wigged out. Maybe everyone around me had.

"You actually believe that? You believe that that old woman can predict her own time for dying?" I asked.

I brought my right foot up so that I could untie my shoe. I pulled the heel back and slipped my foot in. After repeating the same act with the left foot, I wiped my hands together trying to remove dirt that was not there. When I looked up, I realized that Jean was staring at me, his good mood gone.

"A lot of patients know when it's their time to go." He said trying to be patient.

"I can't believe you just said that Jean. You honestly believe that garbage? Well I don't. Not only do I not believe that, I can't believe we have to run a full code on a ninety-eight year old lady. For what? What is the reason for that?

"Huh? Tell me that. The woman shouldn't even be in this unit. She's a drain on our resources and our time. And now you're standing there talking about her like she has a crystal ball or something."

My mouth was still way ahead of my brain. Generally, I think these kinds of things but I never speak them. He stared at me for a moment.

" You have a lot to learn Mat."

He kept his voice low and he spoke slowly as if he were speaking to a kid. In an instant, I knew what Jean Woods was going to be like as a father. Patient and caring. But I was not a child and his fatherly manner infuriated me.

"All human life is worth saving. This lady maybe old and sick now but she hasn't always been that way. A woman of her years has a lot to offer. She's a historian for one thing for another thing this country was born on her back. So I don't see her as a drain on anything, let alone my time."

I stood staring at him. "Oh that's rich. No pun intended." I said wishing I could turn my mouth off. "Maybe you're treating your guilt. I mean, didn't your family get all of its money from a large southern plantation?"

"Most of it. But I won't be held responsible for something I had no control over. What I will be held responsible for are my own actions. And my actions tonight were to run a full code in the absence of my intern.

"Now I could be chewing your ass out for not responding to a code 99 and for not having a good reason for not responding to it. But I'm not. I don't give a damn what held you up. All I care about is that you're here and that you're all right.

"And now that you're here, you've got work to do. It's almost five o'clock. Labs need to be reviewed, orders need to be written and my advice is for you to start with Mrs. Morris. Any questions?"

"No." I said wanting to say more but I didn't. My brain had finally caught up and taken over my mouth causing my tongue to be tied. For that I was thankful.

"You know Mat, I've heard you refer to me as smug and arrogant several times in the last five days." He said staring me in the eyes. "But let me tell you something, I can't hold a candle to you when it comes to that attitude of yours.

"You walk around like the world owes you something. Well it doesn't. You don't own the market on broken promises or whatever the hell happened to put that chip on your shoulder. If you don't want to be here, apply to another program." At that he turned to leave. I stood alone shaking with furry

"Why are you really here Jean?" I asked before he went through the doors. He stopped and turned back to me.

"To keep you from screwing up." He said taking a step towards me. "See you're my responsibility and I know your heart ain't in it." At that he turned and was gone.

As much as I hated Jean and I hated him a lot, he was right about everything. My heart really wasn't in this. So what? I thought. I didn't need for my heart to be in this to get through it. All it takes to get through this program is half a brain. I was already ahead of the game there.

I walked to the table outside of room six. Without looking in, I sat down and read over Sadie Poole's notes. The code had been nothing more than a scare. No drugs were given, the patient wasn't intubated nor did she ever stop breathing. She appeared to have lost consciousness but only for a moment.

I looked at the monitor. Her heart rate was seventy-four, her blood pressure was stable. Point made. She didn't need to be here.

If this patient had been on the floor, she would have had this little episode unknown to any one. Instead, she's a full code and the whole hospital had to be turned upside down for nothing. Anger at this woman replaced the fear I'd felt earlier.

I needed a break. I knew I was being stared at and talked about and quite frankly I'd had enough of it. Without looking in on Mrs. Morris or looking at any one else, I left the unit.

I took the elevator to the first floor. Using the ER as an express way, I walked out to the ambulance ramp. Once there, I took in a deep breath of fresh air. I was alone and loving it. It was how I preferred it anyway.

While enjoying my solitude, a thought occurred to me. Maybe I wasn't being fair to her. Was there really nothing left in life for her because she was ninety-eight.

"Okay lady help me to understand." I said under my breath.

I thought about what her life must have been like. She was old and black. It couldn't have been that great, I thought but I tried to give her a reason to live anyway.

If I were ninety-eight years old, what would I want to live for? What is it I would want to do that I hadn't done already. Nothing. If I were ninety-eight and I hadn't done it then it wasn't to be done.

So I thought about family. Maybe she was holding on for a son or daughter we didn't know about. Maybe she needed to make a phone call. Maybe there was someone who didn't know that she was in the hospital.

But how could that be? She was found in an abandon house. If she had family, they didn't seem to care. Even if she was in a nursing home and had wondered away, the family would have been notified. Once she was found, you would have thought the family would have been right there to make sure she was okay. Or seeing how much they could sue for. Something.

No she had no family. I was sure of that. Not the way the media plays on the heartstrings of this country. Her family would have been found if there was any.

Maybe she's outlived all her family. I thought about that. That was a possibility. But why struggle to hold on if that was the case. Even if she is made of stern stuff, there comes a time in everyone's life that one must realize that its time to throw in the towel. That the battle is not worth fighting for.

Then I thought about her health. If I were ninety-eight years old and healthy, doing for myself, getting around on my own then I could see fighting. But her health is lousy. Even if her mind has the will, her body doesn't. Age is going to be the victor no matter how hard she fights.

Even if she wins this battle, she's already lost the war. She'll be dependent on someone from now on. My health and my mind are all I've got. If I lost either of them, I'd have no reason to live.

She has no health and based on the question she asked me earlier, she's not dealing with all her faculties. So what is she fighting for? Why hang on when there is nothing to hang on too.

"Okay lady. I tried to understand. But there is nothing and no one."

At five minutes after five I headed back. I went back through the ER. Everyone was so busy no one seemed to notice me. Once in the ICU, I noticed again that everyone was busy. Too busy. I seemed to go unnoticed again.

That was okay with me. After the little confrontation that Jean and I had earlier, I was happy to go unnoticed. The last thing I needed after all that has happened tonight was another confrontation.

I sat down so that I could look over Mrs. Morris' chart again. Nothing had changed in the short amount of time that I was gone. I really hadn't expected it to. I just wanted to prolong going into her room for as long as I could. But I had reached the end of that prolonged period.

I'd put off the inevitable long enough and could think of no other reason to put off going into her room. It was time to make the donuts. Her heart rate was seventy-four. BP was now 108/52. That's better than most. I thought.

I was not prepared to look directly at Mrs. Morris. I was afraid of what I'd see. Looking at her monitor was safe.

I swallowed and realized I had a lump the size of a small apple in my throat. I was afraid and I couldn't stand it. What's more it made me angry again? What could this woman do to me? With that thought fueling my courage, I looked in her room but only at the wall opposite me.

I saw my reflection in the window. I looked stupid even to myself. So I had to look stupid to those around me. Jean had been worried about me. I was worried about me too.

I looked at Mrs. Morris. I just looked at her without thinking about it. The longer I thought about it, the easier it would be for me to talk myself out of looking. So I just did it.

I screamed at what I saw. Seeing what had frightened me was why I'd been prolonging the inevitable. There looking back at me were those eyes. No face! No body! Just eyes!

I closed my eyes. When I opened them, I looked to see what kind of crowd I'd attracted. No one. Not a single person had come out to see why I'd screamed. In fact, I found that I was the only person in sight.

I looked back at Mrs. Morris. Her eyes were looking back at me. The way she appeared to be nothing but eyes made me think of Alice and Wonder land. But the cat in that story had been eyes and a smile. She had no mouth.

The hair on the back of my neck stood up and I fought back another scream. Again, I closed my eyes. When I opened them, I felt foolish. There looking from her deathbed was a fragile old black lady. She was no more dangerous now than she'd been when I saw her earlier in the night.

I looked at my watched. It was five fifteen. I was way behind so I decided to get this over with. I stood on wobbly legs, with knocking knees and I went into Mrs. Morris room.

"Hi." I said. "Remember me. I um..." I said then stopped. I cleared my throat and started again. "I hear you gave everyone a scare."

I gave up on trying to be cheerful and decided to just get down to business. She wasn't answering me anyway. She simply lay with her eyes closed and she sighed. After a moment of silence, I felt my confidence growing. I asked myself again why I'd been afraid.

I stood staring at a ninety-eight year old black woman that was as harmless as a rabbit and probably just as frightened. I looked at her eyes. They were closed but there was nothing unusual about them. I couldn't explain what had caused me to see what I'd seen. It didn't matter now because whatever it was, was gone.

It was my turn to sigh. "I need to examine you Mrs. Morris." I said but I didn't move.

I stood staring at her waiting to see what would happen. When nothing did, I took a step towards her. Then she spoke.

"If you had looked behind your book bag, you would have found your shirt." She said. "You look a mess child."

Her eyes remained closed but they were moving rapidly from side to side behind her closed lids, as if she were dreaming or watching movement.

I stopped at the sound of her voice. My chest got tight. My head felt a little dizzy and objects in the corner of my line of vision started to fade.

"You better breathe before you pass out child." She said looking at me.

I did as I'd been told. It was like I was almost afraid not to. Maybe she did have a crystal ball. She certainly knew things she couldn't possibly have known without one.

"Matthew Allen why don't you come on in and sit down. You and I have something to talk over." I shook my head and backed up until I bumped into the wall. De`ja`vu! There was nothing I needed to or wanted to talk over with this woman.

"That kind of thinking could hurt a person's feelings." She said. Her comment confused me but I didn't say anything. And I didn't move.

"Matthew Allen time is growing short." She said very serious now.

"How do you know my name?" I asked.

"I know many things child. Far more than one person should know." Was her answer.

"Who are you?"

"Jean was hard on you out there but not hard enough." She said not answering my question. "You can't go through life not caring. You don't have to love everyone you meet but you need to care about someone other than yourself."

That did it! "I beg your pardon." I yelled. "You don't even know me." I found defending myself helped. Anything was better than being afraid.

"What right do you have to say that about me? Furthermore, I don't appreciate you butting into my business. And another thing…" I said looking at nothing but large white eyes again. I shut up. No amount of anger could get me past those eyes.

"I can take care of myself." I said almost afraid to speak. "No one…" I stopped still looking at those eyes.

"No one cares about me." She said finishing my thought. I stood still seemingly glued to the floor and nodded.

"Why don't you like me Matthew Allen? Because I'm black. Because I'm old. Because I scare you or all of the above."

I looked out the door unwilling to look at her. "I don't like or dislike you Mrs. Morris. I simply think you being in this unit is a waste of resources." I couldn't believe I'd said that. Thinking the truth was one thing. Speaking it was another.

"You don't like or dislike me? Is that what you tell yourself about every patient you take care of? Isn't that what you tell the young ladies that you've attempted to have a relationship with?

"Isn't that what you tell the people that try to become your friend? It is, isn't it child? You tell yourself that so you don't have to like Jean or Sadie Poole or anyone else for that matter. See Matthew Allen, I'm aware of what's going on here. The problem is, you aren't. And it's time to put an end to that."

"And just why do I tell myself that?"

"I'm afraid you have to figure that out for yourself."

"In other words you don't know."

"You think helping me is a waste of your time. Don't you Matthew Allen? I don't think that about you."

"Why should you?"

You're incensed at the thought that I, a ninety-eight year old black lady, could think of you as a waste of time? Aren't you? Tell me why I shouldn't think that?"

"You tell me why you should." I challenged.

"Okay I will. For starters Matthew Allen, you're like the grinch. Your heart is two sizes too small and you've never given anybody anything. Me, I'm always giving. In fact, it's why I'm here."

"Yeah right. You know what? I'm busy. I don't have time for this nonsense. I've got a lot of work to do and I'm already behind. So…." I stopped, put my watch to my ear and listened.

I heard a steady tickticktick. My watch was working but somewhere along the line it must have stopped. It read five fifteen. I looked at the clock on the wall. It too read five fifteen. I stepped to the door and looked out at the clock hanging over the nurse's station. It read five fifteen.

First the eyes now the clocks. Personally I preferred the clocks but none of this should be happening. How was any of it possible? I wondered feeling a spell of vertigo starting.

It was five fifteen when I came in the room. That was at least ten, maybe fifteen minutes ago. I double-checked all three-time pieces again then noticed Sadie Poole outside the door. She sat down so that she could write in the chart that belonged to the patient in room seven.

"Mrs. Poole my watch seems to have stopped." I said standing in the doorway so that she could see me. "Can you tell me what time it is?"

I knew whatever time it was it meant trouble. Trouble because I was behind and this lady's unwillingness to cooperate was making it worse. I could see myself trying to explain all of this to Jean Woods. I didn't dwell on that thought for long because it dawned on me that Sadie Poole had ignored me.

"She can't hear you." Mrs. Morris said. I didn't want to or maybe I wasn't ready to deal with that so I ignored her.

"Mrs. Poole." I yelled. "Sadie!" When Sadie Poole didn't respond, I looked back at Mrs. Morris.

"You can't keep ignoring me child."

I wanted to say, 'watch me.' But I was struck by an intense feeling that warned me not to say it. Somehow I was sure that making that comment wouldn't be a good thing to do.

"Okay." I said turning back to her. "What do you want? Why do you want it and what does it have to do with me?"

If she could answer all those questions, it would at least take us straight to the issue at hand. She could get whatever it was on her chest, off her chest and I could get out of her room and back to the things I had to do.

I didn't have time for the game she was playing. Game! Could that be it? Was this some kind of game?

Or maybe it was test. Could they be testing me to make sure I could cut the mustard so to speak? I've never heard of such a thing but anything was possible.

"The only game being played here Matthew Allen is the one you insist on playing."

I looked at her shocked by her comment. She was reading my mind. That thought was so maddening that I tried not to think about it.

"Mrs. Morris my name is Dr Green. I'm your doctor and I'm here to take care of you."

I wanted this woman to respect my title no matter how many years there were between us. I was so frustrated by the fact that she was calling me by my first and middle name, something that she should not have known, that I actually stomped my foot. I wanted this conversation to be over. I wanted to put a stop to the nonsense that she had insisted on. Instead of giving her a reason to respect me, I found that my actions made me look more like a spoiled brat than an educated man.

"Your not doing a very good job…at taking care of me that is."

"I'm doing the best I can. I'm…rather new at this." I said then stopped. What in the hell was I doing explaining myself to this old black lady.

"My, my aren't you hostile. You don't like the truth do you? Well here's something else you're not going to like. To take care of a person, one must care. You're doing such a lousy job not because you're new but because your heart ain't in it. You did agree Jean was right about that didn't you?"

I didn't answer. She really was reading my mind! She had to be because there was no way she could have known what Jean and I had discussed. There is no way she could have heard that conversation either. It had taken place all the way on the other end of the hall. Before I could come up with an answer, she spoke again.

"Did I keep you up tonight?"

"No, not really. I got some sleep."

"There's more to life than sleep you know."

"Tell that to someone whose sleep deprived and I'm sure they would disagree with you."

"You're not sleep deprived. You just don't care."

"You keep telling me that. You're starting to sound like a broken record."

"Do you know why Jean Woods gave up a night of sleep to be here tonight?"

"Yeah, because he's the resident. Ultimately everything falls back to him."

"Pity you're so jaded and at such a young age. But I guess you didn't get this way all by yourself." I stood with my back against the wall and sighed.

"You bored child?" She asked then laughed.

"Actually, yes." I said challenging her.

"I'll see what I can do to change that Matthew Allen. Or would you prefer it better if I called you Mat?"

"I would prefer it better if you told me what you wanted! How you knew my name! And how you're able to read my mind!" I yelled.

As soon as I finished yelling, I looked towards the door. I wasn't ready to concede to this woman. I wanted a reason to leave this room. That outburst should have given me what I wanted. That outburst should have brought all the nurses running and I wanted it to do just that.

It didn't. In fact, no one even moved. I looked back out the door and noticed that there didn't seem to be anything amidst. Sadie Poole continued to sit outside of room seven. Instead of charting, she was now labeling blood bottles.

"What's going on here?" I asked Sadie Poole but she continued to ignore me. "Oh I get it. I'm dreaming. Is that it? Am I dreaming?" I asked turning back to Mrs. Morris.

"Pinch yourself and see." She suggested. I did and the pain I felt was quite real.

"Besides why would you be dreaming about a ninety-eight year old black lady that has nothing to offer? That is how you see me right?" In my own defense I said nothing.

"What do you want?" I ask not knowing what else to say.

"Believe it or not, I'm here to help you."

"I don't..."

"Need your help." She cut in and finished my sentence. "Yes, yes I know. You feel you don't need anyone don't you child? Not Jean Woods, certainly not the Grandma Morris's of the world."

"That's because I don't. I've gotten this far without anyone's help and I'll continue the same way. Now if you'll excuse me..."

"How did I know your name Matthew Allen Green? That is the question you've been asking yourself. That and a few others. But that one for sure." She asked looking at me and shaking her head.

I must have been wearing her out because all of a sudden she sounded tired and old. I looked at her. She lay looking back at me waiting for an answer. I looked at her monitor. I noticed her heart rate was still seventy-four. I looked at my watch then at the clock over the nurse's station. How was she able to control time was a better question.

"I don't know." I finally said. All of a sudden I knew this thing was bigger than her just knowing my name.

"You told me. Oh not with your mouth child but you told me none the less. You also told me how unimportant I was to you. That I should realize I wasn't going to live forever and to go on and die. You told me all of that."

"I never said anything like that." I had felt it sure but I never gave voice to it.

"You also told me." She continued to say as if I hadn't spoke. "That because I was old I had nothing to live for. More importantly, you told me I have nothing to offer.

"You decided all of that for yourself. You've never met me before tonight. You don't know where I've been or what I've done. Before tonight, you didn't even know I existed but you decide what was best for me because it would make your life easier.

"That last part really hurt me. For you see, I have only one thing to live for and only one thing to offer. And the very person I 'm living to offer it to doesn't think I'm worth his time. That's pretty damn ironic if you ask me."

I leaned against the wall again and stared at her. What was she babbling about? She had nothing I wanted. I wanted to say this but I didn't. If I had, I would only have been proving her right.

She sighed and looked away. "You don't have to take what I'm offering you Matthew Allen. I could go back to where I came from empty handed. There is no shame in being wrong.

"Not everyone's heart can be touched. I don't believe that about you though. I believe you're worth the time and the effort regardless of how you feel about me. I want to help you."

"Okay, look, I did think and feel those things about you." I said. I wanted to say I didn't mean any of it but I couldn't. Since I was confessing, I felt compelled to confess all. But to do so would only hurt her more. "I just didn't think the unit was the place for you. That's all." I said instead.

"Considerate of you not to want to hurt me. That's the first time you've allowed yourself any humanity in sixteen years." She said.

"Huh?" I asked. "Who are you?" I asked taking a step closer then taking that same step back.

"Who I am isn't important. What I am is. What I am is ninety-eight years of memories and experiences. And I want to offer that to you. " She said.

"And just what am I supposed to do with that? Write a book! I already know about the black experience. As Jean Woods told me earlier, I'm not responsible for your people being enslaved. I wasn't even born!"

"This has nothing to do with slavery Matthew Allen. At least, not the slavery you speak of. By the way, do not compare yourself to Jean Woods because unlike Jean, you refuse to be responsible for your behavior."

"What do you want from me?" I asked.

I was tried of being picked apart by this lady. Standing before her, I felt as if I'd been sent to the principle's office. I had done nothing wrong and I was tired of being treated as if I had.

"It's really quite simple child. I want to touch your heart. I want to show you why you don't care. I want to show you why you should care.

"After that, I want to show you someone who did care for you when you thought no one did. I want to give you a place to call your own. There, you will find people who will always care for you. Think about it child, you'll never be alone again."

She spoke slow and longingly. Like she could see what she wanted to show me. Like she wanted to go back to the very place she spoke of. I had to admit I found the place rather tempting.

Instead, I stood where I was thinking this was as good a time as any to leave. It was still five fifteen and her heart rate was still seventy-four. She didn't need me. So I turned to leave. I felt if I didn't let her tell me what she felt she had to, I wouldn't have to make promises I had no intentions of making or keeping.

I tried to walk out the door. With all my might, I concentrated on moving my feet and legs out the door. I turned instead towards the inside of the room. I then walked to the only chair in the room and sat down.

I looked out the window. I saw nothing but darkness and that struck me as odd. I was in a fairly large city so all that darkness made no sense. Somehow, I felt like I had been teleported from that thriving metropolis to a rural setting. There seemed to be no streetlights. If there were lights, they were not strong enough to penetrate the black velvety darkness that surrounded them.

All the units are located on the third floor yet somehow I felt that I was on the first floor of some building and that building was not the hospital that I came to take call in. The darkness and the influence this lady was exerting on me were interfering with my perception.

"I like being alone." I finally said.

"Yes child that is what you keep telling yourself. It explains why all your relationships are doomed before they are started. It keeps you from getting hurt. It allows you to throw the first punch. That is how you think of it isn't it? Look Matthew Allen, as hard as it maybe for you to accept, getting hurt is a part of living. If there weren't some rain in your life you'd never appreciate the sunshine."

"Oh now there's a good argument. It makes me want to run right out and get hit by a car." She sighed and closed her eyes again.

"That's not what I mean and you know it. But then you always were a wise ass weren't you?"

That comment made me snap around to face her. She was right. I was always getting in trouble when I was a kid for some prank, practical joke or comment made to my sister or mother. Dad would talk to me, warn me never to do it again then he would crack up. I smiled at that memory.

The two of us would have a good laugh because once I promised not to do something, I kept my promise. Dad knew that, which is why it was possible for him to laugh at my adventures. He knew I would never do anything to hurt anyone. God I miss my dad.

My dad has been dead since forever it seemed. Thinking about him wasn't going to change that. Thinking about him in this old lady's room was something I refused to do.

I stood with the intentions of just walking out. If I didn't think about it, if I didn't try, I could leave. Some way or another I was giving this lady whatever power she had over me and I refused to give her anymore. I was sure that was how she was holding me. But I was wrong.

I got to the door and that was as far as I got. It was at the door that my body turned around and came back to the chair. At the chair, I sat back down. All of this was against my will.

I tried to leave three times. Three times I was turned around at the door. Three times I was made to sit down once I was back at the chair. After the third time, I stayed put. It was clear to me I was meant to hear what this woman had to say. Like it or not. I chose not.

"Why should I allow myself to be hurt? That's dumb. That's stupid even."

"Life is a circle child. All life. Everything that lives must die."

"I understand that."

"Yes you do." She said speaking slowly and now in a low tone of voice.

That low tone made it so that I had to pay attention. If I didn't, I couldn't hear what she was saying. Which was really all right with me.

"What you don't understand Matthew Allen." She said without raising her voice. She didn't have to. She was still coming through to me loud and clear. I think she would have even if she had been whispering. "Is why one must endure all the other hurt this world dishes out.

"In ninety-eight years, I've never figured that out and now that my time is near I guess I never will. What I do know is that having someone to talk to and to hold during those crazy times makes life more bearable."

"Why not just avoid it all."

"Because that's not really living."

"But it's my choice."

"That wasn't your choice child. You felt you had no choices. That's why I was sent here. I was sent to show you that there are other choices."

"Why?"

"Because I think there is hope for you. You're still young. If we don't change the course you've chosen you'll wake up one day and find out that it's too late."

"Who the hell am I, Scrooge? This isn't a Christmas Carol." I said. She only stared at me, which caused the hair on my arms to stand up. She was serious and that look made it clear to me that she wanted me to be the same way.

"Okay. At the risk of repeating myself, why? Why do you care? Why aren't you out helping some black intern?"

"Could be the first person that walked in my room in need of my help wasn't a black intern."

"So you're telling me that out of all the people that walked in and out of your room tonight, I was the one with the worst problem?"

"No. You were the only one hurting and didn't know it."

"If I don't know it, what's the big deal?"

"Everything you say and everything you do is affected by your hurt. That's the big deal."

"Whatever." I said shaking my head. "You know what, I don't think you stand a chance but I seem to be your prisoner. Every time I try to leave, I find myself right back where I started. So take your best shot.

"Tell me, old ghost from the past, how are you going to do all of these things? How are you going to 'touch' my heart and make it grow?" I used her own words to mock her and hopefully to anger her.

"You don't want me to write a book but you do want to tell me something or show me something. So do whatever it is you have to do. But get it over with."

"Child you're only twenty-six years old and alone. You're alone because of something someone did to you. And because of that, you have turned your back on everyone who has ever tried to get close to you.

"Until you can figure out why, you're never going to admit that. To do so would mean the end of your defense. The end of your control and we both know that control is all you have."

Not willing to acknowledge what she had said, I looked out the window again. It was so dark and I got the strangest feeling. For the second time, I felt I wasn't in the hospital any more. I stared out the window lost in my own thoughts trying to block out what Mrs. Morris was saying. What did she know anyway?

"I know about the closest." She said shattering my thoughts.

My head snapped around to look at her. My face grew red and hot as if she had slapped me. I didn't say anything. Maybe if I didn't say anything she would move on. Talk about something else. Anything else.

"Matthew Allen do you think two wrongs make a right?"

"You asked me that before." I said in a voice that came from my mouth but one I'd never heard before. I felt something was about to be revealed to me. Something I didn't want to see or want to know and I was scared.

"You never answered."

"Yes I do. Two wrongs make a right. There are you happy?" I asked looking at her. She nodded then looked towards the ceiling. I looked up too.

There before my eyes, in this room, on the ceiling was The Closet. My mouth went dry. My hands became wet and I felt a cold sweat form on my forehead.

"Who the hell are you lady and what do you want with me?" I yelled standing so fast my chair fell over.

I hated her for bringing up that damned closet. I hated her even more for showing it to me. My goal was to tell her that. Instead, I picked up my chair and sat it down in an upright position then I walked to the window.

"I want to sleep child." She said barely above a whisper. Her voice sounded as old as she was. It was more of a croak than a whisper.

"So go to sleep old lady. You don't need me for that. If telling you that is what you needed then there, I have said it. Or am I to do something else, like help you kill yourself? If that's it, then forget it. I will be no part of that."

"No I don't want you to help me die and I don't need your permission. But thank you for giving me permission anyway. I can't sleep Matthew Allen. I can't sleep until I do what I was sent to do. And I was sent to help you."

"But you're not helping me. Don't you see?" I said turning and pleading with her. "Seeing that closet door didn't help me not one damn bit. It can only make things worse."

"Until you deal with what happened in that closet, no one will ever be able to help."

"Oh, so now you're my shrink. I didn't ask you for help. I didn't come to you. Somehow you apparently summoned me." I said.

I didn't like or want this old lady interfering in my life. I was angry now. That was good. Anger was something I knew. In the past when I was angry, I was better equipped to handle whatever was thrown at me.

"It's not me you're responding to. But you're right. When used properly anger is a good emotion."

"What? Are you giving me permission now? If I feel something, you tell me that I'm a good boy for feeling it. Well I don't need you. My life is just fine. Thank you! Everything is exactly like I want it. It's…"

"Not how I want it but it'll have to do." She finished.

"That's not what I was going to say."

"No you weren't but it was what you were thinking. Look child I'm too old to be conned. I've seen the best at work and you aren't even close." I stood staring at her. She stared back letting the silence settle in.

"You don't know nothing!" I said turning back to the window.

The dark was so complete it was actually peaceful and scary at the same time. It was like a velvet cloth had been placed over the whole outside. The only things capable of penetrating that intense blackness were the many stars that lined the sky.

The night sky was beautiful. But I couldn't shake the feeling that something was wrong with what I was looking at. Whatever it was, I knew without being told, that I was no longer in Kansas and the Land of Oz might be more dangerous for me than it had been for Dorothy.

"That's kinda of cute. A good analogy too." She said.

"Get out of my head." I yelled looking at her reflection in the window.

Then out of habit I looked at my watch again. It was still five fifteen. This strange phenomenon no longer surprised me.

"Matthew Allen, I know more than I want to know. My heart goes out to you. What you experienced was a crime. He deserved to be punished. But he wasn't. He dared you not to tell and you didn't. You were so afraid so alone in that closet.

"You did everything a ten year old could do to be good but it was never enough." She said then stopped.

She'd been speaking so soft that I tried humming so that I wouldn't hear her. I didn't want to hear her. When I turned around, I saw that she was wiping away tears. Tears for me.

"I don't want your pity old lady." I yelled through clenched teeth. I knew that she knew what had happened and that made me feel ashamed. I hated her more for making me feel that way.

"How dare you bring up that part of my life? I have worked hard to forget everything that happened back then and in a blink of an eye you dredge it all back up. I never told anyone because I never wanted anyone to know. And here you are, a nobody, putting your nose where it doesn't belong."

At that comment, Mrs. Morris actually sat up in her bed and pointed her finger at me. "Do you really think you are the only person in this world that has been hurt Matthew Allen? Do you think you are the only person that has been mistreated or betrayed by the people that you loved and thought loved you back? Do you think you hold the market on hate, pain and shame? You aren't even close."

There, I had done it. I had succeeded in making her angry and I was sorry that I had. Her voice had been old, tired and soft up to this point.

Now, I watched as she pointed her finger at me. Her voice had a conviction and a strength that belied her frail appearance. I stared at her crooked finger as it pointed at me. It waved and wobbled up and down and her whole body shook from her exertion.

"I'm a ninety-eight year old black woman. I know more about hate, more about being hurt and more about being mistreated than you could ever learn, even if you lived to be ninety-eight three times over. I know the most about hate.

"I hated taking care of someone else's things, nice things then going home and looking at the empty space where I would like something nice to be. I hated the fact that my children were never first to play with their toys. I hated that the best meals I ever served my family were leftovers from the houses I cooked and cleaned in.

"I hated that my best Christmas presents were china patterns or stemware with missing or broken pieces. But more than anything in this world, I hate that my thirteen year old daughter was raped and beaten to death because of a hand me down evening dress that she wore to her coming out party.

"I know hate personally Matthew Allen. I've shaken hands and eaten dinner with him. So don't think you hold the market on that department because you don't. Not now not ever.

"I don't pity you child. That's a wasted emotion." At that, whatever tree she had tapped for strength ran out. As if she were a rag doll, she flopped back in bed. "My heart just goes out to you. That's all." she panted.

For a moment I was quiet. I thought about what she said and I realized she was right. I'd never know or see what she had but that didn't give her the right to stick her nose in my life. I didn't say any of what I was thinking for fear it would set her off again. Then I remembered she already knew what I was thinking.

"Maybe you should save your heart. I'll be fine. I always have been. I'm kinda like a cat."

"You always land on your feet. I know the saying well." She said.

"What is it you said you wanted to do? Touch my heart right? Why? So that you can do what? Save my soul." I asked.

"I'm not worried about my soul." I said. "As far as I'm concerned, there is no heaven and hell is right here on earth. I've been to hell. I survived. As you can see, I'm just fine."

"If hell is here on earth then death can only be what child? Does death just make us worm food?"

"You're the one with all the powers. You're the one that can read minds and dig into people's pasts. You're the one with all the answers, you tell me."

"Talking is getting us no where. I was hoping we could have made more progress by now but time is growing short. Sit. We'll talk later." Against my will I did what I was told. I sat.

"Look at the ceiling child." Reluctantly I did that too.

What I saw made my throat constrict. My chest tightened and I felt faint. I tried to look away but found I was paralyzed. I watched the images until they ceased. Once they were gone I turned my head away and closed my eyes.

Time past before I spoke. How much I don't know. I don't think it was a lot. But I had no way of knowing since it was still five fifteen according to my watch. I was so shocked by what I'd been shown that my brain was on pause. The first question was a repeat of the one I'd already asked.

"Who are you?" I asked fighting back tears and bile.

Both the bile and the tears were fighting hard for domination. I refuse to let either win. I attempted to stand. My legs gave way. They were unable for some reason to support my weight.

Each attempt to stand ended with a heavy thudding sound that my body made when I fell back into my chair. Mrs. Morris lay quietly watching as I attempted to struggle to my feet. I tried not to notice but she was crying again.

After the fifth try, I'm nothing if not persistent, I stopped. I sat panting and sweating as if I had just sprinted the hundred-yard dash. My heart was beating so fast I could see it through my sweaty tee shirt.

"Please explain the point of that."

"You carry too much baggage child. I was sent here to help you remove some of it. As a doctor, you know that sometimes a wound must be opened in order for it to heal. That principle holds true for secrets. A secret is no longer a secret once it has been told or discovered. It can no longer haunt you."

I sat staring at her refusing to wipe the tears away that ran down my face. We both were silent. I'm sure I was suppose to use the time to think about what she'd said but I was too busy thinking of nothing, except who this old lady was.

"To answer your question, they call me Grandma." She told me in a soft soothing voice.

She'd only spoken eight words but the sound of her voice was like a warm whirlpool. It broke up tense spots in me and massaged others. Whoever Grandma was she was capable of a lot of wondrous and scary things.

"You win. Do with me what you must. Is that what I'm suppose to say." I asked.

I was out gunned and whipped. For sixteen years, I'd been running from the truth. A truth I thought only I knew about.

Now, in the earlier hours of this very morning, I was being forced to face my past with a woman I didn't know or like. I refused to trust anyone and with good reason. What made her think I would change that now, I wondered? She let me wonder without answering.

Admitting that I didn't trust anyone proved to me that she was right. It did something else to. Something that totally took me by surprise. It stripped away years of hard work. I've spent the last sixteen years of my life building defenses that made getting up every morning possible.

They made facing smiling couples and cute kids easier. Now all that was slipping away. All that was left was a ten-year-old boy looking through the eyes of a twenty- six-year-old man.

"I'm sorry child."

"Don't speak to me!" I yelled. "I don't want to hear anything you have to say. I never did. I never will." I shouted at her.

She looked towards the ceiling again. I did too. Standing before me was someone I thought I'd never see again. This time I did listen for I was too shocked not to.

"Hi Matty. How are you son? Look son, I'm sorry. I know this is hurting you and I wish I could make you feel better. I wasn't there for you when you needed me. Please believe me when I say I wanted to be there.

"I wish I could hold you until this night was over. I wish I could tell you everything will work out all right. That's really all up to you though.

"I want you to know I'm doing the best I can with what I have. I wish I could give you a magic answer that would make some sense. But I can't.

"All I can do is ask you to try. To do your best. That's all I've ever asked from you son. Don't hate Grandma. She's just the messenger.

"I promise you, if you do your best, when this night is over you will find a new home. You will be a new person. One that you can like and be proud of. One that I can be proud of as well.

"This night won't be easy son. I never said that. Things worth having seldom are. Just hang in there. I love you." Then he was gone. I stared at the ceiling for a moment more hoping that he would come back. When he didn't I looked at Grandma.

"The messenger?"

"The messenger." She echoed.

"Why you? Why not my dad."

"We all have our roles both in life and in death. And to answer your question no."

"What question?"

"I'm not a witch." Knowing it was a childish thought I halfway smiled. She smiled too.

"Why me?"

"Why not you?"

I thought about that for a minute. I couldn't think of one reason someone would want to help me. I wouldn't want to help me if I met me.

"That's why I'm here child. That is the very reason. Understand now?"

"But I already have a family." I said remembering my father's request that I try my best to help Grandma. Before I could help her help me, I had to understand. My father wouldn't want me to participate without understanding first.

"You haven't seen any of them in eight years Matthew Allen."

"I know. I wish I could say I miss them....I don't. We weren't exactly the Partridge family you know."

"No. No you weren't. Most families aren't. You did have one person in your corner though."

Thinking about my father, remembering him standing on the ceiling in this very room made me smile. "He was great wasn't he? I think I look a lot like him. Don't you?"

"Yes you do." She said smiling at me. Then she turned serious again. "But your heart didn't shrink until after your mother remarried. The person I'm talking about stuck by you long after your father died."

"Please! I know you can't be speaking of my dear sweet mother. That woman forgot I was even alive after she married that jackass she married."

"I wasn't speaking of your mother." I looked at her confused. "Who else is there?"

"Well, whose left?"

"Yeah right! My sister was her mother's daughter. First chance she got, she started screwing that jackass too."

"You think that's what she wanted child?"

"She did it often enough." I said. Grandma only shook her head and looked away.

"I see you haven't been paying attention. Matthew Allen how many people knew your stepfather was molesting you?"

"Is this supposed to be a trick question? You know how many people knew."

"Yes but do you." She was getting at something but I could not for the life of me believe Chris knew what was going on.

My father said tonight would not be easy. All he asked was that I do my best so I thought back to the second worse time of my life. As I thought of the events, I was able to see them on the ceiling. I watched with intense interest to see if I had missed something.

I watched as my stepfather made me swear never to tell anyone. He didn't have to try very hard. I wouldn't have anyway. Even at ten, I knew that wasn't the type of thing a person wanted everyone to know. Who would have believed me anyway?

The way most people figured it, Wayne was gold. I remember walking past a group of women one day and I heard them call my sister and me dirty little rats. Remembering that day made it appear on the ceiling.

I watched as the same group of bitches talked in low voices, as we passed by. "They don't know how lucky they are. Wayne Pitts could have any woman he wanted and he chose her with her little brood of dirty little rats."

Maybe he did do us a favor. Maybe he didn't. After my father died, we had it hard. My mother had never worked outside of the house before and she had no skills. Getting a job at a department store was the best she could do.

My mother didn't have a good head for business either. That had been my father's department. So it wasn't long before we lost the house.

I watched as we loaded a hand full of things onto a u-haul. When we were done, that u-haul contained mama's bed, some dishes, a sofa, one overstuff chair and the table and chairs from the breakfast area. The rest the bank made mama sell at an auction. It was an attempt for her to pay off as much of her debts as was possible.

I watched as I walked into that ratty apartment. The walls were in bad shape. Some of them needed painting while others had holes that needed to be repaired.

"Don't worry honey." My mother said to me. "We'll have this place looking like home in no time."

I watched as I nodded. I wanted to be brave and strong. I walked away from my mother trying to feel cheerful. I walked through the two bedroom one-bath apartment that had only four hundred square feet and instead of being brave, I started to cry.

I couldn't understand why my father had left us to live like this. Back when I was eight, I guess I really didn't understand death. Not until my father died. Then I didn't want to understand.

I watched as I stood in the bedroom that Chris and I were to share. It wasn't big enough to turn around in. I know, because I watched myself turning in a circle. Just as I was doing that, Chris walked in and I hit her by accident.

I know she had to hate having to share a room with me. Now I can understand why. But when I was eight, I thought it was kind of great. Chris was a good sport about it all. She never complained. She never made me feel like I was in her way or anything like that. She really was great.

Oh boy. I thought. Chris really was cool. How could I have missed that? Why wouldn't Chris know? I looked at Grandma.

"Is that what you wanted me to figure out?"

"Chris actually did know child." She said. I wanted to argue with her but I didn't. I had missed something so I went back to thinking.

Chris was great, my mind repeated. I thought everything about my sister was cool. I thought my sister was gorgeous and she was smart. Smarter than Mom in many ways. At least she knew how to make out a budget. After we moved into that little apartment that helped.

I remember one morning we were all getting ready to go to either school or work. Mom was in front of us calling to us to hurry up. I was the last to be ready as always. When my mother opened the front door, she stopped and stared. I watched mom, Chris and myself standing in the doorway of our tiny apartment. We were staring at where the car had been parked. My mother closed the door, went to the sofa, sat down and cried.

That was the first time I'd ever seen my mother cry. She didn't even cry when my father died and for a long time I was angry with her. I felt her lack of tears meant she didn't love him. Seeing her cry over a car scared me. It meant losing that car was worse than losing my father.

Like the buzzard that he is, Wayne Pitts started coming around after we lost our only means of transportation. Without that car, mama couldn't get to work. Without her small income, it wouldn't be long before we found ourselves on the streets.

Good old Wayne made it possible for her to get the car back and he helped her get a better job paying more money. Of course, that meant that she now worked for him. I watched her sitting in her new chair, behind her new desk, in a job she was not qualified to have.

I watched the ceremony in which my mom married Wayne. As Mrs. Pitts, mama found she didn't have to work any more. She could spend and spend and never get in trouble. She found Wayne was able to give her far more material things than my father ever could and she seemed to forget that material things weren't the same as hugs, kisses, and family. Because she seemed to have no time for either.

Today, most women would have seen it coming. My mother didn't. She was too occupied with the new house and all the new clothes and furniture that she could buy. My mother had only one job.

I watched as she found out what that one job was. "Darling, as Mrs. Pitts there's only one thing you have to do, just smile and look pretty. No matter what you hear, no matter what I say always smile and look pretty. Do that and the sky is the limit for you. Understand?"

To prove she could handle the job, she smiled very pretty indeed. To show his approval, Wayne patted her butt. Watching them made me want to puke.

In all fairness to Wayne, he was okay to mama. It was me he couldn't stand. Whenever mama was away, he was always on my case. Whenever mama was around, he was all laughs and jokes. It confused me.

After the first year, he stopped even bothering to pretend. I watched the ceiling as Wayne grabbed me by the arm, slap me upside my head, for what reason I couldn't remember. I watched me looking back for my mother. Surely she wasn't going to stand for this. But she stood for that and so much more.

That night my mother came to my room. I listened to her now as I had then. "Honey you just need to stay out of his way. He works hard so that you can have this nice room and all the things in it." She said waving her arm around the room for effect.

"Just stay quiet and out of his way. Things will be okay. You'll see." She kissed me on the forehead. It was the first kiss from her since moving in with Wayne.

I didn't learn to hate my mother that night but I should have. There was more of a message in what she was saying that night than I could ever have imagined. But I was only ten. I was still learning.

As a result of Wayne's abuse, my grades started suffering. I stayed in trouble at school in other ways too. Of course, Wayne had an answer for all of that. I balled both fists and clenched my teeth when I heard his next words.

"I won't have him embarrassing me." He yelled to my mother.

I had just walked through the door. I had been trying to find a way to tell my mom that I'd been suspended from school. I was hoping she'd tell Wayne. As it turns out, I didn't have to tell either one of them. The school had already told them.

I'd gotten in a fight. I don't know why. I can't even remember who I'd gotten in the fight with. It didn't matter in those days. I was always pissed off. All it took was a look and I wanted to fight.

"I will not allow him to goof off around here while he's out of school either." Wayne was saying, "When this week is over, I bet he'll think long and hard before getting into trouble again."

At that, he grabbed my arm and dragged me to the closet at the end of the hallway. At that point, I dropped my head. I'd watched just about as much as I could stand. I stood up and walked to the window.

The goal here was to find out how, when or even if Chris knew. Grandma tells me she did. I say she didn't. I was about to just rely on her word when my father's words echoed in my head.

"Tonight won't be easy. Things worth having seldom are." I sighed then sat back down.

"You'll be allowed out to eat twice a day." Wayne was saying. "At that time, you'll be allowed to go to the bathroom. Don't ask to come out for anything else.

"When you are out, you will not speak to anyone nor will anyone speak to you. You will be allowed out at bedtime. You will take a bath and then you'll go straight to bed. You will use this week to bring your grades up. Understand?

"If any of these rules are broken, I will add another week to you punishment. You understand that?" I watched as I nodded. Then I was pushed into that closet.

If my mother tried to change his mind or my punishment, I wasn't aware of it. I wasn't being shown any scenes in which she tried. I didn't think she had when I was ten. At twenty-six, I now know she hadn't. I spent the whole week in that damn closet. I followed all of the rules. I thought I was a good boy.

And I did learn some valuable lessons that week. None of them had anything to do with school. I learned that the less I ate, the more comfortable I felt in that small closet. I learned to drink less, which made it easier to hold out until the next bathroom break.

Everything I learned that week was about self-preservation. I learned to like being alone. But what I learned to do that was more important than anything else was to hate my mother.

Being in the closet that week was awful. That's because I didn't know just how awful things could get. I would learn though. Over the next three months, I was in and out of that closet for reasons no one could tell me.

No matter how hard I tried, I was always doing something wrong. My grades became straight A's. That wasn't good enough. My hair was too long so I cut it. That wasn't good enough. I finally realized I wasn't good enough.

I watched Wayne as he entered the closet that first time. He said nothing to me at first. He just stood staring down at me. Without warning, he reached down, grabbed me by my arm and pulled me to my feet. I dropped my head. I knew Chris hadn't found out by opening the door and looking in.

"Pull your pants down." He said taken his belt off.

I didn't move for a moment. I was trying to figure out what I'd done to have him come in. When he had his belt off, he folded it in half. I was about to get a whipping. At least, that's what I'd thought.

I was mortified. I'd never been spanked in my life. I never gave anyone a reason to want to spank me. Some of my jokes probably should have gotten me a swat on the bottom every now and then but they hadn't. My father never raised his voice at me let alone his hand.

I was only ten so I did what I was told. What happened after that is the reason Grandma was sent to me. The abuse went on for five months without end.

One day Wayne came to the closet like he had done so many times before. On the ceiling, I saw Chris. That day she'd still been home. Chris was standing midway on the staircase looking for something in her purse when she heard the closet door open and close.

She frowned and looked over the banister. When she didn't see anyone, she frowned again and started down the stairs. She was at the front door when she heard me cry out in pain.

She came to the door ready to break the rules and ask if I was okay. But once she was at the door, she heard Wayne caught in the thrones of passion. The images on the ceiling disappeared.

Wayne's abuse went on for another month after that. I never knew why Wayne started coming to the closet and I hadn't known why he'd stopped. I didn't care why. I was just glad that he had stopped.

"Matthew Allen" I heard someone say. I didn't move. I couldn't move. "Matthew Allen." I looked in the direction from which my name had come.

"There is no way Chris knew about what happened in the closet. If she had known, she would have said or done something to stop him. Wouldn't she?" I asked no longer sure of anything. "She would have done something." I said with a little more conviction. "The Chris I knew and loved would have done something to help me. She would have?"

"She did child." Grandma said softly.

"No she didn't!" I yelled. "What did she do?"

"What do you think she did child?"

"Nothing!" I yelled then stopped. "Oh no. Not that. Oh God no! Please don't let it be true." I cried. "No God damn it! No!"

"Still think two wrongs make a right?"

"Jesus Christ." I said placing my hand over my mouth.

I wanted with my life for this lady to tell me that it wasn't true. When she didn't say it wasn't so, I place my head in both my hands. I cried so hard that I felt like I was going to shake apart.

I'd been wrong about Chris. I'd accused her of being a whore and I'd been wrong. So terribly wrong.

I didn't answer Grandma's question. I couldn't. I didn't know. I didn't know anything anymore.

"She went to your mother but never told her. She tried but your mother refused to hear her out. After a while, she saw that she was only making things worse for you so she stopped trying. It was then that she did the only thing she could think of to protect you.

"If you'll remember, Wayne stopped coming to the closet just as abruptly as he'd started coming. In fact, he stopped sending you to the closet all together. You may not want to admit it but you did wonder why."

"I did. But I was glad to be out of the closet. I was glad he wasn't hurting me. I was so glad that I was not willing to look a gift horse in the mouth."

"You should have. Gift horses have a way of coming with high prices. Your mother realized that too late."

"And just when was that?" I practically hissed.

My eyes and my face were wet from my tears. My nose snotty. I hadn't seen or spoken to my mother since I was eighteen.

"When she found out she had cancer." Grandma said.

Whack! Jesus Christ! Things just kept getting better and better. I thought. It was still five fifteen and already I felt as if this lady had slapped me on two separate occasions. I pulled my head from my hands so that I could face Grandma. "And neither of her kids called or came to see her." She finished.

I looked away. I thought again that this night was not going to be easy. Things worth having seldom are. I wanted this night to be over. Unfortunately, I knew that it had only just begun.

I knew that because Grandma hadn't given me directions to the place that she and dad spoke of. I had not earned the right to go there yet either. I had not been touched yet. I was feeling something but I still didn't care.

I took a deep breath before speaking. "My mother has cancer?" The shock in my voice was real so was my pain.

"Had." Grandma said even more softly than she had spoken before.

That one word was by far worse than any slap I could have received. That one word was like a weight. That one word weighted a ton and it was sitting right on my chest. That one word took my breath away and I sat struggling to breathe.

I didn't want to ask any questions. I didn't want to say the words for fear saying them would make them come true. So I just thought the question.

Is my mother really dead? Can it be true? If it is true, why wasn't she standing with my father a few minutes ago? While it's true I haven't seen my mother in eight years, I didn't want her to be dead. Is it really true that she's dead?

"Yes." Ruthie Mae Morris, bearer of bad news and all around witch said. She took a deep breath and closed her eyes.

I knew without Grandma telling me that her heart went out to me. That made me wish I hadn't called her a witch. I was sure she really hated bringing all this bad news to me. I knew she hated hurting me or my father would not have asked me to work with her. I trusted my father. He was the only person in my life that never did anything to hurt me. He and Chris that is.

Besides, I could see that she was miserable. She had to be. Her knowledge was tearing me apart. That was not her goal. If she wanted to hurt me, why go to all the trouble of trying to help me.

This was her job. A job she had to do. A job she had been sent to do. But she didn't have to like it and I was sure that she didn't. For the first time since being drawn into this room, I understood Mrs. Morris a little better.

"Thank you?" She said.

I nodded and tried to smile. The dimples refused to participate. That was the second time I'd been unable to smile for this lady. The effort made Grandma smile anyway.

"If it helps, your mother wasn't alone when she died. Christine held her hand until the end. With much prayer, Chris was able to find the strength she needed to forgive your mother and she went to her. They got to spend three hours together before your mother died." She said then looked at the ceiling.

I looked up in time to see Christine slowly walking down a hallway that led to my mother's room. She took a deep breath before entering. She was afraid of what she would see and so was I. Turns out, we had good cause to feel that way.

What we saw surprised us both. The woman lying in that hospital bed was not our mother. The lady in that hospital bed was all skin and bones. The cheekbones were too high and too visible. The lips too dry. The skin too pallor. All the beauty was gone. Yet somehow it was our mother.

Chris and I had the same reaction. Utter shock. Both our mouths fell open and our tears rolled. It was the first time that I realized how much Chris and I were alike. Not just in looks but our actions were a lot alike as well.

Indecision kept Chris standing in the doorway. She would have stood there forever had my mother not opened her eyes and noticed her standing there. When my mother saw her, she smiled.

That smile. She'd always had the most wonderful smile. It had healed many a booboos when I was growing up.

Not cancer or death could change that. That smile transformed those high cheekbones, those sunken eyes and those dry lips into a shadow of the woman I once knew and loved. Still loved, if I was honest with myself. Right now I was being honest.

I dropped my head and cried. I'd never get to tell her that. I let the years and my hate take that away from me. I held my head back and I literally howled. The hurt and the pain were so intense that I could not contain it any more. My body needed a way to release what I was feeling. Howling was what happened.

The ceiling was blank when I finished. I looked over at Grandma and I saw her wet cheeks. She had cried with me. Something told me before the night was over I would cry with her again. Then for her. Tonight won't be easy. Things worth having seldom are.

"Can I see more please? I mean did my mother ask about me? Did she want to see me?"

"Yes she did child." Those words were like music to my ears. "Was Wayne there? I mean did he support her?"

"Yes." Good I thought. He was scum but she needed him and he had been there for her. That counts for something. "Can I please see more?"

I watched my mother as she held her arm out to Chris. The way it waved and wobbled reminded me of how Grandma's arm had done when she had gotten angry with me. Her fingers were nothing more than bones with skin wrapped around them. Her palm pale.

The invitation was all Chris needed. She ran to our mother. In the process, she dropped the flowers she'd been carrying.

"Mama." Was the only word she was able to say. She let the bed rail down then got into bed with our mother and held her. They both cried.

"Oh Chris. Oh my baby. I was so afraid I would never see you again." Our mother said in a voice that was so soft and weak that it trembled. "Thank you so much for coming. I've missed you so much my darling.

What could I have possibly done to make you and your brother not answer my calls?" She asked.

"I know I wasn't the greatest mother in the world but was I really that bad. Did I hurt the two of you that much that I made you hate me?"

"It doesn't matter now mama. It doesn't matter. I'm here and I'm so sorry it took me so long. Please forgive me Mama." Chris said. Mama's weak hand wiped at Chris' tears.

"Forgive you?" Our mother asked shocked by the fact that Chris thought she needed to be forgiven. "Chris I love you. I love you and Matthew. If anyone needs forgiveness, it's me. Did he come with you?" She asked.

She knew that I hadn't but she'd hoped anyway. Chris didn't say anything. She just shook her head.

"Chris I know I don't have long." She stroked Chris' cheek then her hair.

Chris didn't say anything. Instead, she held our mother as if she was a scared little girl. Chris looked into our mother's eyes and knew that she spoke the truth.

Our mother's time was indeed close. I knew it because Grandma had told me. Chris just knew it. Chris always had a way of just knowing things. She could never explain how she knew. She just knew.

"I need to know what kept you and your brother away. Tell me what it was that I did." My mother pleaded.

"Mama." Chris said but my mother put a gentle finger to her lips, silencing her. "Where's your brother Chris? Do you know?" Again, Chris shook her head. "He hates me. Doesn't he?" Chris didn't move. She couldn't lie to our mother. Not on her deathbed.

"That's what I thought. Do you know why?" Again, Chris didn't move. "Tell me."

"I can't. It's not my place to tell you."

"Your loyalty to your brother is commendable. I wish I could say the same thing about me. I have racked my brain trying to figure out what I did. The only thing I can think of is he never forgave me for marrying Wayne."

She looked to Chris for confirmation or denial. Chris simply closed her eyes. That reaction confirmed my mother's worse fears but for the wrong reasons.

"I know your brother loved his father. We all did. But Wayne was always there for us. He helped us out in bad times and I love him for that. I love him period. Is that a crime Chris? Is that what made me a bad mother?"

"Mama, marrying Wayne isn't what Matthew is angry about. He knows how much Wayne helped us. He knows that without Wayne we would have ended up on the streets. Nor does Matthew hate you for loving him.

"Whatever happened between Mat and Wayne will have to come from Mat or it will have to come from Wayne. But know this mama, none of it matters now. None of it can be changed and none of it's going to make you better. So let it go. I have."

"Very well put Chris." I said.

"You have?" Our mother asked in surprise. Chris' comment let my mother know there was something that someone needed to be forgiven for without telling her who or for what reason.

"Yeah mama. That's why I'm here. I love you. I forgive you. Now why don't you forgive yourself so that you can rest?" My mother positioned her head so that she could get a good look at Chris. She nodded then smiled.

"I don't deserve you. You know that?" She said pulling Chris to her so that she could kiss her. "Will you do me a favor? Will you tell Matthew that I love him? Tell him I love him so very much." Chris nodded. Then Wayne came into the picture. And my mother turned her attention to him for a moment.

"Did you do something to hurt them honey?"

"Darling don't you fret so. Everything will be okay. All that matters is you. Relax. Just relax. I'll answer for whatever sins I may have committed when the time comes." Mama started to say something but Chris stopped her with a very firm voice.

"Mama knowing won't change anything. If anything, it will only add to your pain. And I think you have enough of that right now. Whatever happened, happened. Let it go. Please." She kissed our mother's cheek. "Please."

My mother nodded and smiled that smile of hers. I filed that smile away in my memory so that I would not forget it. What other choice did I have? I was never going to see it again.

She and Chris snuggled together and thirty minutes later my mother looked up at Chris. "Keep your promise okay? And remember that I love you." Then she took a deep breath and died.

"Chris tried to reach you but couldn't." Grandma said.

"That's how I wanted it." I said finding away to turn off my feelings. I felt nothing. I didn't want to feel anything. I was numb and I liked it.

I was never going to see my mother again. I was never going to get to hold her or hear her tell me she loved me or that she was sorry. But that was all right. Sorry wouldn't be enough anyway.

"Your are a stubborn one."

"Her husband fucked my ass!" I spit. "What do you want? What do you expect? Am I supposed to say it's okay? I hate that my mother has died. I hate that she was in so much pain but she wasn't there for me when I was in pain so it's only fitting that I wasn't with her through her pain.

"All my mother needed to do was pay attention. All she needed to do was stay home once and a while. All she needed to do was talk to us and she would have known something was wrong. But she was too busy being Mrs. Wayne Pitts.

"I'm not here to defend your mother. But forgiveness is part of moving on." I ignored her. I didn't want to hear any of that garbage. There was something more important on my mind.

I was thinking of all the time I had missed with Chris. I didn't know where she was. I didn't know if she was married or if she had kids. All I knew was eight years had been wasted.

"Why didn't Chris tell me she knew? It's possible that with both of us going to our mother and reporting the abuse she would have believed us."

"Chris did the best she could. She was only sixteen. She didn't have all the answers either. She tried to figure things out. She tried to figure out what would happen to the family if she told someone what was going on.

"Things were a lot different sixteen years ago. Sexual molestation was reported less than now and believed even less. Especially when the charge was against someone of Wayne Pitt's social status. Chris decided if the two of you reported what had happened, the worse that could happen was that you guys would be back where you started. Except now, your mother would hate the two of you. The least was no one would believe you.

"She tried to see people believing the two of you. She tried to figure out how to support the two of you on her own. In the end, she decided the best she could do was run interference. She hated being touched by that man. But she loved you just as much as you remember her loving you."

"Where is Chris, Matthew Allen?"

"I don't know." I said softly.

"Matthew Allen, as your father told you, there is a place for you. I want to offer you that place. It'll be a place that you can call your own.

" I want to lead you to a family that will help you deal with the loss of your mother and your childhood. They will accept you even when you're at your worse. There is no mystery here child.

"All you have to do is allow yourself to feel. You have to trust someone other than yourself. You have to believe that everyone you meet is not out to take advantage of you. Matthew Allen I'm just asking you to care.

"Let me see if I can touch your heart. I know you have one. I just saw you using it. But just as soon as you opened the door you closed it back."

"Grandma am I dying?" I asked, thinking that could only be why all of this was happening.

"No child. But I am."

I thought about my family and how they had let me down. I thought about my father asking me to do my best. He asked me to make him proud. Then I thought about Chris and how I had let her down. Maybe I could take her with me.

"You could." I looked at her. I hadn't spoken the words but I liked the answer.

I was quiet for a moment thinking hard about all I'd learned. "I've had sixteen years of practice. You know, of not caring or trusting." I said doubtful. "What if you can't reach me?"

"I can. The method used will seem unorthodox to you, even brutal but I can reach you. I know I can because I believe in you."

"Your time is short."

"I believe in you child."

"I don't."

"Good. You just made my job a lot easier. Admitting that is a start. Two hours ago you wouldn't have done that."

"What makes you think these people will want me."

"Because I want you."

"That's it."

"That's it. Once you tell them I sent you, they'll know you can be trusted. That you've changed. But most importantly they'll know I was able to reach you."

"I see." Not sure that I did. "What do you get out of this?"

"To sleep child." She said not belaboring the point.

"Help me to understand some of this. How are you controlling the time? How are you able to produce memories from the past? And how is it that you are able to read my mind?"

"Tools of the trade. I'm just the messenger. I'm not capable of anything." She said then stopped as if she was thinking. "Do you remember watching the Ten Commandments when you were a child?"

"Yes."

"That's how it is with me. God spoke through Moses. I'm not saying I'm Moses mind you." She said laughing. "I'm just saying I was called upon to do a job. In order to get the job done, things happen. It's five fifteen because that's what time you entered this room."

"Am I awake?"

"Yes."

"But no one knows I'm in here."

"That's correct. I don't know how any of this is done. And I don't want to know. Mine is not to question why."

"The eyes what did they mean? That you see all."

"Very good child."

"You like Jean Woods. Why didn't you offer this to him?"

"Jean is already blessed. He already has what I'm offering you."

"You keep asking me about two wrongs making a right. Why?"

"Does it?"

"I don't know." I said shaking my head. I stood and went to the window. All that seemed to exist now was darkness. No stars. Just darkness.

"You're thinking what if you trust me and I screw you over. Like everyone else has. You want to trust me because your father told you to but what if I conjured him up. What if it wasn't really him? That's a good point Matthew Allen.

"When you trust a person, you have to trust them because you want to. Not because someone else did or because someone told you to. You can trust me child. Tonight is not going to be easy. Things worth having seldom are. It's good you keep remembering that. It is so true."

I laughed then ran my fingers through my hair. It wasn't a laugh of joy but a nervous laugh. A laugh that you sometimes heard people use right before excusing themselves from a room.

To my own ears, this laugh sounded like the one crazy people used on TV, right after having a nervous breakdown or having unloaded a gun on a crowded room of people. But laughing was better than crying. I feared if I started crying, which would have been more appropriate, I was sure I would never stop.

"You're not losing your mind Matthew Allen. If anyone should be losing his or her mind, it should be me. See child, I know things about you no one else knows.

"The only way for that to happen is for me to have spent some time with you in that closet. I tried to claw that son of a bitch's eyes right out of his head." At that I laughed again. My eyes filled with tears as I looked and listened to Grandma.

"God doesn't allow that kind of talk does he?" She smiled.

It was warm and full of love. For me. Like my mother's smile, it told me what Grandma had once looked like as a young women.

"What about the monitor? Your heart rate hasn't changed from seventy-four since I got here."

"That's the year that you will be going back to. Nineteen seventy-four."

"Umm…the year I'll be going to?"

I wanted to think that there was nothing left to shock me. But there was. I had not been prepared for that answer. I wanted to ask more questions but I looked at her monitor instead. The alarms were going off. They shouldn't have. Her rate was seventy.

"The count down has begun." She said looking at the monitor.

"Whoa! Hold up a minute! I don't understand. Are you telling me your time is based on your heart rate?"

"Yes."

"Oh. No problem." I said confidently. "Seventy is a strong heart rate."

The monitor alarmed again. This time her heart rate was sixty-eight. This made goose bumps stand out on my arms. "I take it business is at hand. No turning back?" I asked.

"No turning back. Please be seated." At first I didn't move. When her heart rate dropped to sixty-seven, I did as I had been told.

"I participated in the killing of two men." She said then lay quiet. When I didn't say anything but sat in shocked silence, she continued.

"It was July sixteen, nineteen seventy-four. A very beautiful young lady from my hometown was expecting her first baby. Bonnie was her name. She and her husband Lawrence were counting down the days until their little bundle of joy would arrive.

" So was the whole town as a matter of fact. See, the people in my hometown watched Lawrence and Bonnie grow up."

As Grandma spoke of Bonnie and the expected baby, her face changed. Slowly a smile started across her lips. The more she spoke the wider her smile grew. Seeing her smile was like watching an amazing transformation.

Slowly, the lines diminished on her face until she somehow looked younger. As I watched her, it became apparent to me again that Grandma Morris had once been a very beautiful woman too.

"As the two of them grew, they became the best of friends." Grandma continued. "Then they fell in love. We all anticipated the announcement of their engagement, the wedding and finally the news that they were pregnant. At the end, we were all counting down the days until the delivery.

Watching Grandma, I relaxed. I crossed my legs and even found myself smiling with her. I found that I was no longer mystified by the outside but comforted by the total darkness that seemed to surround us. I was no longer worried about the time, although it remained stuck at five fifteen. What did worry me was her heart rate.

At sixty beeps per minute, I knew she was not long of this world. This scared me. She had a hell of a job to do and I didn't want her to run out of time. Plus, I found I no longer wanted her to die.

As an intern, I knew a heart rate of sixty marked the beginning of the normal scale. In Grandma's case, however, it placed her one step closer to zero. One step closer to death. I looked from the monitor back to Grandma. For some reason, she'd gotten quiet again.

The smile on her face was slowly disappearing. As if she was releasing it against her will. Her soft sweet voice once filled with joy and promise was gone when she spoke again.

"The day of celebration was not meant to be." She said then took a long deep soulful sigh. "She was only twenty-two years old. So young. So beautiful. She had her whole life to look forward to. They both did.

"It seems as though the two of them had waited all their lives to be together. All they got were two years."

My attention had wandered back to the window. When I heard that the two of them only got two years together, I looked back at her. It wasn't until then that I understood how her heart rate came into play.

For it was when she told me the two of them had only been allowed to spend two years together, that I realized her heart rate was set with her telling me this story. The more of her story she told, the older and more tired she seemed to get. Telling this story was killing her. Literally!

Her speech was slow as she spoke of Bonnie and Lawrence. I heard the tears that sat at the edge of her voice. From where I was sitting, I saw that there were tears at the edge of her eyes. When she sighed again, I knew the tears had already started spilling over the edge of her heart.

She was hurting. She didn't have to do this. She wanted to do this. And she was doing it all for me.

I dropped my head and fiddled with the cuff of my pant leg. I felt ashamed of myself. I hadn't treated this lady too kindly. If I was honest with myself, I still didn't fully trust her.

How could I? I didn't know her. I don't know what she has in store for me. I still can't prove that she didn't make my father up. Lord knows she didn't make the closet up.

I was struggling. For her sake and mine, I needed to find a way to trust her. I needed to learn how to care. I needed to do all of this in the space of anywhere from a few minutes to a few hours. I wasn't sure I could do that. Yet there she was hurting.

I tried to remember what it was like to trust. What I remembered was trusting Wayne and dropping my pants. I expected to be spanked. I trusted that, that was all he was going to do. Even if I didn't know why. Instead, he molested me.

She had said forgiveness was part of moving on. How could I forgive him for that?

"I didn't ask you to forgive him child. But you must accept that it happened. You can't go through life trying to forget or pretend it never happened. Deal with it.

" When I asked you to forgive, I meant yourself. Forgive yourself because you could not stop the molestation from happening. Forgive yourself because you did not cause it to happen."

I sat staring at her. "I can't do this. I'm sorry. I know the clock has started counting down but I don't want to go through with this."

"You have to now child. The count down has started. I'm going to die when this is all over. What happens to you is up to you. Just try."

"Things are going to get a lot worse than anything you've already showed me, aren't they?

"Yes they are. But you will never be in danger. You have to trust me on that."

"You used the word brutal."

"This night won't be easy child. Things worth having seldom are." I nodded at her.

I was scared but I would just have to deal with it. "You were telling me about Bonnie and her baby." I said.

"She was going to be a teacher." Grandma said smiling.

Her heart rate was now fifty-eight. Even with her time being short, she seemed to be just as reluctant to tell the story as I was to hear it. It seemed she wanted to remember the good things about Bonnie before having to tell me about the bad things that happened to her.

This only added to the fear I felt. She was dying. Yet knowing this, she was still struggling with what she must tell me.

"She loved kids and they adored her." Her speech was slow and loving. "Bonnie's idea of the perfect future was to be with the kids in her class all day then go home to her own kids and husband.

"It looked like her dreams were just about to come true too. She had a year to go before she graduated. She was going to teach grades one through three at our own elementary school. But she didn't get to do any of that though." She said then sighed again. Fifty-six on the monitor.

"On July sixteenth two despicable men cut her life short without a thought or care. I say men but they weren't much more that boys."

She looked at me then out the window. She appeared to be looking at the two men even as she tried to describe them.

"One was twenty-one the other was only nineteen years old." She said. "They were despicable because their hearts were filled with hate. Their hands covered in blood.

"They were drifters with no job and no intentions of finding a job. Everything they wanted, they took. No matter the price. What made these two even more despicable was the fact that killing was nothing more than a game to them.

"The two of them would sit in a large parking lot and wait. They were looking for a target. Generally, their target was old and black. Being black was the only real requirement.

"If their target wasn't dressed to shabbily and if their target's car wasn't too old, that won them the prize. The prize was having their ass kicked; their brains beat out of their head, their car and valuables stolen.

"Once that was done, they'd write on each mirror 'I just rid the world of one more nigger.' If they liked the car of the new target, they would take it. They weren't afraid of being caught or anything like that. They knew the police weren't taking these cases serious.

"What they were afraid of was being spotted by someone who might know one of their targets. The police might not have been taking the cases serious but the black community was and we were scared. These two knew that fear made people dangerous. To avoid trouble, they switched cars whenever they could.

"When they chose Bonnie, it wasn't because she was driving a nice car. She wasn't. She caught their eye because she was so beautiful. They thought spending the afternoon with her would be fun.

"The only qualification was already met. When she went through the drive through at the bank, they figured there was still money to be had." Again, Grandma got quiet. She looked at me then out the window then back at me.

"Are you alright?" I asked. She laughed.

For a moment, she reminded me of me when I thought I was losing my mind. There was no humor in her laugh just like there had been none in mine. I felt she was scared. Just like I was.

I had the feeling she wanted to be anywhere but here. Just like I did. I felt sure she wanted to be doing anything but what she was about to do.

I felt sorry for her. Then I remembered her getting angry with me earlier when I accused her of feeling pity for me. 'Pity is a wasted emotion.' She had said. I didn't want to pity her but I didn't know how to make my heart go out to her.

"Child I've seen and heard so much over the last ninety-eight years that I'm guaranteed to never be alright." She answered. "Never. See Matthew Allen, I was there the day Bonnie was killed and there wasn't a thing I could do to help."

"You were there?" I sat straight up in my chair. She had my full attention now.

"I was there just like you will be." At that she looked at the ceiling.

"Uh…what do you mean?" I asked feeling like I had missed something. How did we go from her telling me a story about her friend, to her watching that friend die, to me watching that friend die?

When she didn't answer, I tried to speak again. My throat was too dry. I attempted to speak twice before I was able to complete the mere act of swallowing. I opened my mouth but nothing came out. I repeated the act of swallowing then I opened my mouth again. I was surprised when words actually came out.

"You told me Bonnie died in nineteen seventy-four. How..how…I mean." I stammered.

"Watch." A one-word command that made me break out in a cold sweat.

"Oh God." I groaned.

Somehow, I knew that as bad as my experience was in The Closet, it was going to be a picnic compared to what Bonnie went through. I didn't want to see what happened to her. I refused to watch.

I turned my back to Grandma, dropped my head to my chest and closed my eyes. There was no way I could see the ceiling. Immediately, her monitor started alarming. I closed my eyes tighter, so tight, in fact, tears formed and slowly rolled down my cheek.

Did I want a place to go bad enough to look at the secrets that this lady had carried in her head and heart for twenty-five years? I decided definitely not. Then I saw Chris standing in the hall. Instead of letting Wayne in The Closet, she took him by his hand and led him away.

My answer went from being a definite no to yes. I owed Chris. I don't remember opening my eyes. I don't remember turning my chair back around. But I must have. At five fifteen a.m. I looked towards the heavens only to be introduced to hell.

Part II

BLINK! Without warning, I found that I was no longer in Grandma's hospital room. I was outside. Not outside exactly.

I was in a moving car. Literally in a moving car. Not looking at the ceiling. Not watching a moving car on the ceiling but actually in the car.

I was so shocked by this turn of events that I found I was having a hard time breathing. Then I realized that it wasn't all shock that was making it so hard for me to breathe. The inability to breathe was also due to the intense heat I felt all around me. The car that I was riding in was like an oven with a warm breeze blowing through it.

In the blink of an eye, I went from the comfort and safety of an environment that I knew in 1999, to an environment that I didn't know twenty-five years into the past. My initial reaction was not to believe. Yet a moving, hot car was a long way from a cool hospital room. I thought about opening the door and jumping out. The car wasn't moving fast and Grandma did tell me I would not be hurt during this, this…adventure.

Common sense and better judgment prevailed, making me realize that jumping from a moving car was stupid. I knew Grandma had no intentions of hurting me. That, however, didn't mean I was exempted from acts of stupidity of my own doing.

I needed air though. Since it was best that I stayed in the car, I did the only thing I could do. I stuck my head out the window. This improved my condition a little but I was still far from comfortable.

"Okay Mat, what to do?" I asked.

The only answer I came up with was to get a handle on where I was. It would help if I knew how long I'd be here but for starters finding out where here was, was a priority. My second priority was figuring out how to deal with my situation until things improved.

I filled my lungs with hot air and remembered that I was a Boy Scout once. In that organization, I was taught to be prepared for anything. "I can handle this." I said. I'm sure there is nothing in the manual about taking a leap backwards into time. But how different could the seventies have been?

They had electricity in the seventies. They had air conditioners in the seventies. Okay this car doesn't have one but there were cars in the seventies that had air.

Feeling much calmer about things, I stuck my head out the window again. This time so that I could get a good look at the road signs. I had to be dreaming. There was no way around it. This whole thing was a dream.

I knew this for a fact because I saw the road signs but was unable to read any of them. The right side of my brain had taken over. It's a known fact that the right side of the brain is at work when you are dreaming. That's why you can't read.

"Is that a fact child?" Grandma asked.

"Yes it is Grandma."

"Not this time Matthew Allen. You won't be able to read these signs until you've earned the right to read them."

"Oh." I said.

"There are no secrets here child. Stop working so hard. All you need to do is relax."

"Relax! You've sent me twenty-five years into the past and you want me to relax?" I asked but I got no reply,

Great! "Okay so I don't know where I am."

That was okay. I think. I was still connected to Grandma and she knew where I was. There were things I did know. I knew that it was July 1974. I knew that it was hot and if I don't figure out what's going on soon, Grandma is going to die and I am going to become Scrooge.

"Okay Mat, so you're scared. That's acceptable. Thinking stupid thoughts, however, is not. Nor will it help. Get serious." I told myself.

Since I didn't know where I was, I decided to narrow things down and at least figure out who was driving the car. I knew I was sent here to learn how Bonnie died. I think I was even sent here to see if I could save her.

That's the part that really scared me. What if I couldn't save her? What if after doing everything possible, I could not save her. What then? To avoid looking at her, I took a better look at the contraption she was driving.

The interior was gray and clean. The outside looked to be a dark blue or maybe black. It was hard to tell from inside the car. The dash was cracked. The steering wheel had a well-worn cover on it, which was used to protect her hands. Her hands? That confirmed my suspicions and I had no choice but to look at her.

It was Bonnie. Grandma had been right. She was indeed beautiful. At first, I could only see her profile. Even then, I could see that her skin was smooth and silky. Her cheekbones were high and prominent. Her eyelashes just the right length for giving butterfly kisses.

Over the years, I've heard several descriptions used to describe black people. Descriptions such as pecan tan or the color of a perfect cup of coffee. I had never used any of them myself. Describing someone meant that I would have to use my time to look closely at someone. I didn't care to look or get that close to anyone. For me, knowing a person's name was more than enough.

I took the time to look at Bonnie. What else was I to do? I was riding with someone that I knew was going to die. That knowledge alone was enough to evoke a sick kind of morbid curiosity.

Bonnie looked both ways before turning left onto a street. I could see the name of the street and actually knew what the street name was but for the life of me I couldn't read it. It was like having the name of something on the tip of your tongue but not be able to say it.

When she turned, I saw her full face. She had big, dark brown eyes. The kind that guaranteed she got her way whenever she wanted. At least, I would have let her have her way if she wanted it.

"You accused me of not caring Grandma. You never accused me of being blind." I said hoping for a response. I needed to know Grandma was still there. I got no response.

Bonnie could have been a model. Not for makeup though. She had no flaws to hide and there was nothing that could be used to make her look any more beautiful. In fact, she wasn't wearing make up now. She was just beautiful. To paraphrase a well- known prose 'that face could launch a thousand ships.'

She had long straight dark brown hair. In a darker light it would have been black. I reached out to touch it then stopped. I was sure I wasn't meant to do that.

I watched her as she drove. Her arms were long and thin. Her fingernails were short and unpolished. Her lips were full without a trace of lipstick. Had our paths crossed in another lifetime, I think I could have, would have fallen in love with her.

Or would I? That is why I'm here. Isn't it? Had I met Bonnie yesterday, full of life and unmarried, I never would have spoken to her. I would have noticed her just not invested any time in getting to know her.

"Oh God." I thought and ran my hand through my hair. Maybe I have been walking around with blinders on. I looked out the window then back at Bonnie.

I remembered Grandma telling me that Bonnie had been pregnant when she was murdered. I looked at her abdomen and saw that she had on a maternity top. If she was pregnant, I didn't see it.

Most of the pregnant women I've examined seem to become one big round center when they are close to delivery. Not Bonnie. In fact, she showed no signs of being far enough along to be wearing that maternity top let alone counting down the days until delivery.

I looked away. She was going to die soon. A woman, who had everything to look forward to in life, was at the point of actually seeing some of her dreams come true was going to die.

That same woman was sitting in the car with me. Or rather I was sitting in the car with her. It didn't matter which way was correct. She was going to die without seeing any of her dreams come true.

I didn't care so much about the fact that she was going to die. As Grandma said, death was a part of living. What bothered me the most was the uselessness of it all. If that's a step towards caring then I was on my way. But somehow I didn't think it was.

I squinted out the window at the houses and other cars that we passed to keep from staring at her. The sun was bright and hot. It was shining through the windshield at full force, making it that much hotter and that much more difficult to breathe.

I leaned my head back against the headrest trying to get comfortable. In this position, the glare from the windshield was worse. Without thinking, I reached for the sun visor and pulled it down.

The sudden movement surprised Bonnie, causing her to scream. Her scream caused me to scream. Our reaction caused us both to feel more than a little stupid.

She gave a nervous little laugh then a glance at the visor. I did what I thought was a smirk, sucked my teeth, shook my head then leaned against the headrest again. Once she completed a right hand turn, she glanced back at the visor.

"This old car is just falling apart." She said shaking her head then pushed the visor back up.

Afraid of what would happen if I pulled the visor back down, I left it where she'd placed it. As far as I was concerned, I was in enough distress. Not being able to see, breath, make out where I was or cool off only added to that distress.

"Damn it Mat! You're doing it again." I scolded myself.

This woman is going to die and I cared for nothing more than my own discomfort. Oh Grandma, I fear I will fail. If I fail, you will fail. That was something I didn't want. It was something I couldn't let happen.

It was something, one of the few things in fact, I really felt strongly about. Grandma was hurting. She was dying. On top of dying, I couldn't let her fail.

I had to try harder. I had to do my best. So this wasn't easy. Things worth having seldom are. With that, I tried to relax.

As soon as I relaxed, something occurred to me. I cared about something. No, I cared about someone.

"Damn it Mat." I hissed through clenched teeth. "You sure have lousy timing. The one person you care about other than yourself will die when all of this is over." I leaned back again.

This time to wait and ponder what I was feeling. How could I have known? The very person I turned my back on, the very person I felt unworthy of my time is the very person that saw that I was drowning.

Tagging along with Bonnie took me first to the Fast Fare Pump and Shop convenient store. At first, I wasn't sure why we had stopped there. But I sat quietly and watched as Bonnie pulled up to a pump. She tried to fill a tank that was already full then headed for the door. My goal was to sit and wait for her return but found that wasn't part of the plan.

BLINK! Without having opened my door, without having gotten out of the car, I found myself walking along side Bonnie as she entered the store. I walked with her right up to the counter where she tried to pay a red haired cashier named Grace one dollar.

"Grace, I'm so sorry. The gauge must not be working. I thought I was close to empty. Lawrence must of filled it up and forgot to tell me." She said. She seemed to be uncomfortable by her encounter with Grace, like maybe she was afraid or embarrassed.

I looked at her. What was going on? She and I both knew the gauge was working. Why was she lying?

"No he didn't." Grace said coming from behind the counter smiling. She and Bonnie hugged for a moment. "You were checking up on me. Now weren't you?" Bonnie just stood there. She'd been busted.

She started to say something then changed her mind. Lying wasn't one of her strengths. They both knew it.

"Yeah. I'm sorry. I was just so worried about you. You haven't been to church in two weeks. You haven't returned my calls. Grace I didn't know what else to do."

"I'm sorry I made you worry Bonnie." Grace said putting her arm around Bonnie's shoulder. "I've just had a lot on my mind. Been trying to work some things out. That's all."

"You're not thinking about going back to him are you Grace?" Who's him? I wondered. What was this stop all about?

"Bonnie, I know you can't understand this but I loved that man for fifteen years. Still do, I guess. He wasn't always mean to me. He just got that way. Here lately I've been feeling guilty. I've been feeling that he needs me now more than ever. For better and for worse you know. I feel I'm letting him down."

"Grace, he beat you up!"

"I know that. One time in fifteen years! The man got drunk, came home, took his anger and frustrations out on me. If he hadn't been hiding the fact that he had lost his job from me, he may never have exploded. He didn't think he could tell me. I can't help wondering if maybe I put too much pressure on him."

"Grace his not telling you, his going out and getting drunk, those were his choices. Don't blame yourself for that."

"Bonnie you are so young, so sweet and innocent. I hope you are always like this. I hope you never have anything happen to you that will change this part of you. Thank you for caring. Thank you for coming by. I promise, I won't make you worry again."

Grace looked at Bonnie then kissed her forehead. "I'm lucky to have a friend like you. Now you take this dollar and buy that baby something from his Aunt Grace. You hear me?"

Bonnie looked as though she was going to say something else but didn't. What was there to say? I'd never seen Grace before today but I knew she was lying. I was sure Bonnie knew she was lying too. But arguing the point would serve no purpose. So she didn't.

Watching the two of them, I noticed that Grace must have been at least ten years older than Bonnie. But the two didn't seem to notice the age difference. They stood talking as if they'd been good friends all of their lives. I wondered how that was possible. We were talking the seventies, where tolerance was a better way of describing the relationship between whites and blacks.

Instead of simple tolerance, these two women loved each other. I watched them as they talked. Grace seemed to be tired. Not work tired but worn by life tired. I looked into her green eyes. Those eyes would have been nice to look into if they only had some life, some light.

While Bonnie and Grace were talking about the baby and how the nursery was coming along, Joe Waters interrupted them. He seemed to be recovering from some kind of accident. I wasn't informed as to what had happened but his arm was in a sling.

I was surprised and a little angered by what I was allowed to know and what I wasn't. I figured only the things that were going to be useful to me was made known to me. Things I wanted to know went unanswered.

While Joe was still there, Martha Bird came in. I shouldn't have known Martha or Joe. I did though.

Martha had been in some kind of accident as well. Again, I didn't know what had happened to her but I knew that like Joe and Grace for that matter, she had been injured. I'm betting her injuries were at the hands of someone she knew. I'm also betting that maybe it wasn't really an accident.

Then there was Billy. Billy Whitlock was one big bruise. He waved when he came in because he was unable to speak. Broken jaw.

What in the world happened to him, I wondered? When I got no answer I got frustrated. I didn't just want to know bits and pieces. I wanted to know everything.

To make matters worse, Bonnie and Grace did not discuss either of the three after they were gone. But even without them gossiping, it was clear to me that the people of this town were accident-prone. Three people entered the store. All three of them had been injured. It was like the people in this town belonged to the Walking Wounded Club.

I watched as Grace gently placed her hand on Bonnie's abdomen. Immediately, I knew Grace had no children. I knew that she could not have children and I knew why. I wanted to be shocked by the information. I even wanted to care about Grace's misfortune. But I couldn't.

I was a kid! I couldn't fight back! Grace just didn't fight back. Now look at what she has lost. And to think, she's thinking about going back to the creep.

"Matthew Allen, there are a lot of people that would say you could have fought back but didn't. Be careful not to judge, lest you be judge."

I thought about that but said nothing. Could I have fought back? How? I thought of everything and everybody in my life when I was being molested. I had no one to turn to. The one person that did help ended up being molested to.

"What could I have done?" I asked Grandma. It wasn't the first time that I've asked myself that question. If there was something I could have done differently, I wanted to know.

"I didn't say there was anything that you could have done. But when you pass judgement, you piss people off. Those pissed off people are the ones who would think that you had other recourse. If I believed that, I wouldn't be here fighting for you."

"You're losing."

"I haven't given up on you child. Don't give up on me."

"This won't be easy. Things worth having seldom are. Right?" I asked really needing her support.

"Right. You have my support and so much more Matthew Allen." She said.

The end of my conversation with Grandma was also the end of the visit for Grace and Bonnie. "See you at Sunday school?" Grace said.

"I'll be there."

BLINK! I have no memory of getting back in the car. I have no memory of being driven from the parking lot or being driven to the bank. I just looked up and found Bonnie and myself at the drive through of the bank. Stop number two.

There, Bonnie exchanged greetings with Patty Weaver. Patty was another member of The Walking Wounded Club. She was the owner of a long scar that started at her right temple and curved around her jaw line.

Like Grace, Patty asked about the baby and Lawrence. Their little chat went on for ten minutes because there was no one else in line. This gave me a chance to look around.

I still couldn't make out any street signs nor could I read the sign over the bank. I was able to locate a grocery store with a large parking lot though. It didn't take me long to realize where stop number three would be.

According to Grandma, the two were able to spot Bonnie while she was at the drive through. I looked to see if I could make out anyone looking at us. I saw no one but that meant nothing. I was at a disadvantage. The view I had wasn't great.

BLINK! I don't know when Patty and Bonnie finished their little chat. I don't even remember pulling away from the drive through window.

None of that mattered apparently. What was important was I found the two of us parked in a large parking lot across from the bank. Immediately after parking, I spotted two young, white males sitting in a parked car. They were both watching Bonnie.

So these were the two that were going to end Bonnie's life. I opened my door with intentions of walking over to them and telling them I knew what they were planning. Instead of walking towards them, I found myself walking along side Bonnie.

I thought about this while trying to stay calm. There must be a window, a margin of space in time that I'll be able to change the events that happened on this day twenty-five years ago. Now didn't seem to be that time.

There had to be something like that or why would I have been sent. Surely, the main purpose wasn't to just watch her die. Surely, I was not sent here without the ability to do something about her death.

That would be ludicrous. That would be absurd. That would be plain terrifying. What made this even more terrifying is that Grandma had watched her die unable to change events. Why did I think I could change something she couldn't?

Okay I'm scared. That's a feeling. But fear and anger were feelings that never went away. So those two must not count.

"They count child. But you can't go through life being angry and afraid."

"Uh...I was doing just that until you felt the need to change things." I said. I knew now was not the time for that. I waited for her to tell me just that. Instead, her response was the alarm on her monitor.

"Damn it!" I said then looked around me.

Much to my dismay, Bonnie and I had entered the store. Without thinking, I reached for a buggy with the intentions of pushing it for Bonnie. My hand went straight through it. Okay, so I wasn't meant to help. Great. Uselessness was also a feeling I was familiar with.

Unable to help, I went back to thinking of ways to delay or even stop Bonnie from going home right after this little trip. The only thing I could think of was to put something in her pocket. I hoped she would be detained for shop lifting.

If nothing else, the delay may make the two of them frustrated. It may make them find someone else to target. It may even make them leave. I picked up a pack of M&M and placed them in her open purse. I felt confident that this was the answer.

The fact that I was able to pick up the M&M did not escape me. Why had I been allowed to pick those up and not push the buggy? It was a mystery to me but if this saved Bonnie's life, it was a mystery I didn't have to know the answer to.

"Matthew Allen why does everything have to be a challenge for you?"

"I don't understand."

"Figure it out child. Time is running out."

"This is a challenge. Isn't it?"

"You will have many challenges in your life child. This isn't one of them."

"Then, I was sent here to watch her die. Not to do anything about it."

"You were sent there to find your heart child. That's all."

I thought about that. Okay, so I was sent here to find my heart. Did that mean I was to do nothing? I couldn't just sit back and go along for the ride. I just couldn't.

"Why not? Because you care."

"No! Because I'm a civilized human being."

"This isn't going to be easy. Things worth having seldom are." She said.

I hated that saying. I've recited it and heard it so many times that if I heard or said it again I was going to choke on the words.

I turned my attention back to Bonnie. She had loaded the buggy with about fifty dollars worth of odds and ends. What caught my eye more than anything was the steak and all the fixing. She was planning some sort of celebration.

BLINK! Just like that I knew what the celebration was about. She had been to her OB doctor. There, she'd been given an ultra sound and pictures. She was having…just like that my knowledge was gone. I was not allowed to know the sex of the baby.

"What's the big deal?" I yelled. My feelings were slightly hurt.

I hated this. One minute I knew people I'd never met. The next minute, I couldn't be told what had happened to them. Now, I knew that Bonnie had been to her doctor but I could not be allowed the knowledge of what she was going to have. I was tired of being jerked around.

"None of this is about you Child. Try to keep that in mind. You will be told all that you need to know. The rest is not important right now."

"Like I said, I'm tired of being jerked around." The alarms went off again. I didn't want to know what her heart rate was. It wasn't good no matter what it was.

One thing was impressed upon me while we shopped. Bonnie was well liked. Loved was more like it. A trip that should have taken no more than twenty minutes took one hour and thirty-two minutes.

Every turn we made, there was someone asking about her, the baby and Lawrence. The whole town seemed to know Bonnie, her little family and they were all in this one store at the same time. I've not seen anything like it since I was a kid living at Wayne Pitt's house. The whole town knew him well too. Or they thought they did.

The very thought of Wayne made all my thoughts of Bonnie and her crisis disappear. Hate filled my heart and I balled both my fists. This was not going to work. I couldn't do this.

"Grandma! Please bring me back. I can't do this. I'm sorry. I can't get past Wayne Pitts."

"Matthew Allen if you don't get past Wayne Pitts, you won't be any better than him. His assault on you was nothing but his hate for himself and his life. Past and present. Is that what you want."

"What are you saying? Because of my hate for him, I'll molest my son, my daughter or both."

"No child. I'm saying you won't have any children at all. Matthew Allen at the rate you are going, you will end up old and alone. Is that what you want?"

"I like being alone."

"We don't have time to go over this again."

"Just bring me back!" I yelled.

All I heard were alarms but they weren't to Grandma's monitor. Bonnie and I had just walked out the door. The alarms were to the security system. Good, this will make her stay longer. There's no way those two idiots are still out in that hot parking lot waiting for her.

"Hi Bonnie." Buddy Sands said. Another walking wounded. He had a long scar under his neck. Someone apparently had tried to cut his head off. At least it looked that way.

"Hi Buddy. I don't know what's buzzing. I paid for everything." Bonnie said. She blushed, embarrassed by the events.

"I'm sure you did." He said smiling. "Your purse is open. Maybe something fell in it by accident." He said pointing.

Bonnie gave Buddy her bag. He half- heartedly went through it. When he found the M&M, he pulled them out and handed them to Bonnie.

"I swear I didn't put those in there Buddy."

"Walk through the door now and see what happens." Buddy said, giving her back her purse. She did and nothing happened.

"Okay sweetie, have a good day." Buddy said then turned to walk away. Halfway in his turn, he turned back to Bonnie, who was still standing in the doorway. "Where are my manners? Can I carry those for you?"

"I got it. Thank you." Bonnie said still embarrassed. "Buddy I swear I wasn't trying to steal."

"Bonnie, even if I thought you were and I don't, I'd buy them for you. So don't you worry about a thing. Buddy's not. You just have a good day. Okay?"

"Okay." She smiled and hurried out the door.

Just as we walked out into the sunlight, I saw the black Cadillac drive pass us. My plan had almost worked. A few minutes more and Bonnie would have lived to see at least another day. At the sight of Bonnie, they braked turned left and parked. There they waited.

"Jesus Christ!" I yelled. "Thanks a lot Buddy! Thank you for being so understanding. Now these two are waiting for her again."

I ran my hand through my hair. I refused to believe Grandma was right. I had to believe that there was something I could do. So I tried to think of something else.

Then it hit me. I grabbed for Bonnie's bag. My plan was to pull it from her hand. Buddy was still watching. If she needed him, if he walked her to her car, would they leave? My hand went straight through the bag. Bonnie kept walking.

I ran back to the store. I wanted to give Buddy a reason to come out of the store. I wanted him to pay closer attention to Bonnie and the parking lot. More to the point, a black Cadillac. The door wouldn't open for me. I stood in front of it waving like an idiot. The next thing I knew, I was standing beside Bonnie as she loaded the groceries into the car.

"I'm trying to keep this woman from being murdered. Doesn't anyone care?" I stood in the parking lot yelling.

"Are you sure you don't care?"

"Grandma, I have watched people die before. I've even been on the team trying to resuscitate them. I'm not afraid of people dying. I just think death at a young age is pointless. If she can die at such a young age then so can I."

"So your concern is about you." I didn't answer her. "Shame is a feeling too child. But it's a negative one. You've felt enough of those don't you think?"

"Yeah. Yeah I have." I said looking at the ground. "Is it bad to want to change things?"

"No child. Why you want to change things is the problem." I nodded. I actually understood that. I didn't know what I was going to do about it but at least I understood it.

The two would be murderers waited until Bonnie and I pulled out of the parking lot then they followed. I thought about what Grandma said. I thought wanting to help Bonnie should have counted for something. My reasons shouldn't have mattered. Helping was the right thing to do. Maybe helping was just my way of trying to stay sane through this whole thing.

Whatever I was doing, I needed to do. I couldn't just sit back. This wasn't a movie I was watching. This was life or in Bonnie's case soon to be death. So I decided I'd keep trying. I needed to do something to keep her from going home. So I touched her arm.

Her skin was as soft and as silky as I had thought it would be. While touching her skin felt good to me, my touch did nothing for her. If she even felt my touch, she did nothing to indicate it.

"Look lady, going home is not such a great idea right now." I said trying to remain calm.

She made no response to my comment. By now this did not surprise me. No one knew I was here except Grandma and myself. It frustrated me but it no longer surprised me.

Instead of responding, she simply looked ahead. Both her hands were on the steering wheel. She hummed as if there was nothing wrong. I guess for her there wasn't. To her, today was no different from any other day.

Well it sure is for me and doggone it, I refuse to continue to work alone. I wanted to help her but I was running out of ideas. Without regards to scaring her, I did the one thing that had worked before. I reached for the visor.

My goal was to flap the damn thing up and down. If I had to, I'd even pull the damn thing off. I touched it tentatively. I was no longer sure what I could and could not touch. It was smooth, solid and hot to my touch. Good I was able to touch it. I was glad to know I had something to work with. I pulled on it.

The impending scream came just as I anticipated that it would. But it came from the wrong person. It came from me. I screamed from both anger and frustration as my hand slipped straight through the visor.

"Sweet Jesus!" I muttered wiping sweat from my forehead, top lip then my hands. "This is senseless!" I yelled into the car. All I got for my screaming was a ringing in my ears. I closed my eyes. I didn't want to see where we were going and I didn't want to know when we got there.

Whether I wanted to or not, my eyes opened when Bonnie slowed the car to a stop. We were at her house. The moment I was dreading was close at hand. I didn't want to be here. No one really seemed to give a damn what I wanted though.

Bonnie drove into the garage and parked the car. After turning the car off, she just sat there humming. She was so happy. She should be. She didn't know hell was about to visit her.

I watched her. She sat holding her abdomen. The life inside of her was stirring. This knowledge produced a sweet dreamy smile on her face as she closed her eyes.

Ignorance truly is bliss. I thought as I watched her. I opened my mouth to tell her she was going to die then stopped. It was no use. Besides, I don't think I could have spoken anyway. My throat was so dry it hurt.

"Why don't you give it up Mat? This lady is going to die. You're all out of ideas anyway. You can't win so what's the point?" I asked myself. "What makes you think you can do what Grandma couldn't do?"

I sat straight up. That wasn't the first time I'd thought that. It was, however, the first time that I listened to it. I'd been lying to myself. Still.

Grandma had been sent to help me. When she asked me to try, I'd said yes to her all the while meaning no. That's why I was still trying to change what had already happened.

That realization sunk to the bottom of my stomach like a brick. All of a sudden it wasn't just Bonnie's survival at stake but my own. I wasn't afraid for my life. I was afraid for my sanity. As before, fear and anger motivated my actions.

"Get me out of here Grandma! I'm sorry if this means you fail. I'm sorry if this means I fail. But I want out of here. I want out now!" I demanded watching Bonnie carry her bags to the door.

"I lied to you when I said I wasn't afraid to see someone die. I never get used to my patients dying. In fact, I hate it!"

"I know that child." She said.

"Besides Grandma this is different." I said putting my head in my lap. "This lady isn't just going to die, she is going to be murdered. Raped and murdered. Right?"

"Yes."

"I don't want to see that." This time she didn't answer. "Grandma!" I yelled. "I know you hear me. Answer me damn it!" Still she was quiet. "You said I could trust you. You said you wouldn't screw me over. Do you remember that? Well I'm bent over and feeling royally screwed!" I yelled.

"Matthew Allen I have not betrayed you. I warned you that this night was not going to be easy, as did your father. You chose to hear what you wanted to hear. I told you Bonnie would die.

"You chose to believe you were sent with another purpose other than the one I told you. I told you there were no mysteries here. You chose to believe that there were. Events have started to unfold. There is no stopping it now."

"You knew what I was thinking." I yelled at her. "You knew what you were saying wasn't getting through to me. You knew." I said crying.

"You told me you were committed. In fact, your last thought was that you owed Chris. Then you looked towards the ceiling. Do you remember that?"

"Yes." I admitted. Lying had already gotten me in way over my head. I didn't want to make things any worse than they already were.

"Matthew Allen, I promised you that you were not going to get hurt and you won't. I promised you that your sanity would not be at stake or in danger and it will not. But child, my goal is to reach you in the short time that I have left. Drastic measures are going to be taken to accomplish this goal. Trust me when I tell you, you won't get another chance."

"Cut the crap Grandma!"

"Anger will only cloud your judgment child."

"I don't like this. I don't want to be here. I change my mind. Reach me some other way. Please Grandma. Get me out of here." I yelled banging my fist against the cracked dash.

My head was down in hopes that I would not be made to see any more. I cried like I was ten again. I shook and slobbered with sheer fear, anger and total helplessness. Then I realized I was no longer in the car. I was in the kitchen.

Bonnie was standing at the counter totally oblivious to my presence, my screaming or my banging. I watched her put away the rest of her groceries. I watched as she took a freshly baked cookie from a rack and sample it.

She was pleased with the results of her baking and finished the rest of the cookie. Today her plans were to go all out for her family. She would make Lawrence all his favorite dishes. And why not? She had good news to share with him. I turned my back to her. I didn't want to see her.

I could hear her and even with my back to her I could still see her. She hummed as she put together a salad. When that was done, she checked on a loaf of bread she was waiting to rise. She reminded me of June Cleaver. She was quite the little homemaker.

Once she was satisfied with the progress of the bread, she took the steaks out of their wrapper and placed them on the counter. She fumbled through her cabinet for a moment until she found the meat tenderizer. Once that was found, she pounded those steaks until she was again satisfied. Then she placed them in a marinade she already had made. I should have just turned around and watched.

"Point made Grandma. She's a loving and devoted wife."

"Is that all you got from that?" She asked.

Jesus Christ! What more was there to get. I wondered. I didn't wonder for long because Bonnie finished with her preparation then she left the kitchen.

I waited to see if I would follow. I did not. So I waited to see if I'd get a vision of what she was doing. Again I did not. I was meant to stay in the kitchen.

I sat there staring at the wall trying to prepare myself. The end was near. I could feel it.

I reached for a plain white napkin to blow my nose. My tears I let dry on my face causing my face to feel tight. Despite the circumstances I smiled.

That's because my dried tears made me remember a time when I was about seven. I'd been playing out by my father's workshop. I was dirty and sweaty but having a great adventure hunting for anything I could find.

It was also July. It was right after the fourth of July but I couldn't exactly remember what day it was. Anyway, I spotted a butterfly sitting in the oak tree right behind the shop. And of course I decided to catch it.

All at once, I was Matty Green, world renowned butterfly hunter. I smiled again at that thought. So had my father when I told him about it later. Anyhow, I grabbed my father's fishing net and I started up the tree. I knew the tree well. I'd climbed it so many times during my adventures that fear of falling never crossed my mind.

What did cross my mind was that butterfly knew I was coming. Cause every time I got close to it, it would move just a little further away. In the end, it took me all the way out to the end of the limb. The limb as it turned out was weak. When I got to the end of it, it simply sagged. I fell.

I screamed in pain and I cried for what seemed like hours. That little expedition bought me a cast for six weeks. What made me remember that were the dried tears on my face.

When I got home, my sister ran to me with her arms out. "Oh poor, poor Matty." She'd said. "Look at how much you've been crying. Your tears have carved two roads right down your face and they lead straight to your heart. Come look and see." She said leading me to the foyer mirror.

"What does that mean?" I asked. Even then I knew my sister was the greatest.

"Well, it means I have to kiss each road so that the tears don't make it to you heart and stay there." She said.

"If tears pile up in your heart, you won't be able to love. All booboos must be kissed away Matty. Haven't I told you that before?" My father asked. I remember nodding.

"Okay Chris you start the healing. Mama you're next then me."

I came away from that adventure totally healed. No tears made a home in my heart that day. But somewhere along the way they had. Nobody kissed away the roads after my father died. There was no one to kiss them away now either.

"Do you want to go through the rest of your life Matty with no one to kiss that hurt away?"

"No Grandma I don't."

"Care child. I see a light. All you have to do is care."

"Wouldn't it have been easier, if you had started me out with someone I know?"

"Easier yes. But there's nothing wrong with caring about someone you don't know."

"No but it's just hard…er." I cut my own sentence off. I let my father's words play in my head.

"This night won't be easy son. Things worth having seldom are." He'd said.

I'd heard those words when he said them but at some point I managed to block their meaning out of my head. I did it because I was so sure I would be able to choose my own path. Now I played those words back slowly over and over finally understanding them. I mean really understanding them.

"Nothing and no one is promised to you child. You take what you've been given and you work with it knowing that tomorrow may never come. Do you understand?"

"I think so. You've sent me to watch the untimely death of a woman who had everything. Everything but a promise of a tomorrow. And she lived each day knowing that."

"That's right."

"And she was happy anyway."

"Not anyway child. In spite of. Just care Matty. You know what? I like Matty. It tells me that once upon a time you were a happy little boy. Full of love, life and promise. I'm gonna call you Matty cause I know that kid is coming back as a man.

"I like Matty too." I said. Then I sat and waited for the next event to unfold. I didn't have to wait long.

From where I was sitting, the living room was off to my right. The back door was off to my left. The door leading back to the garage was behind me. The kitchen was small and cramped.

A couple of steps in any direction could get you to the refrigerator, the stove, the counter or the kitchen table. It reminded me a lot of the apartment I lived in after my father died. The difference, this kitchen was clean and well organized.

A light tap on the back door got my attention. The knock wasn't really meant to be heard. It was simply their way of seeing if there was anyone in the kitchen. When no one answered the door, they tried the knob.

Getting into the house was easy. One twist of the doorknob actually opened the door. After a quick look around, they stepped into the kitchen, closing the door quietly behind them. I stood and faced them. Why I didn't know? They couldn't see me and so far it has been strongly pressed upon me that there was nothing I could do.

Facing these two, I had to agree with Grandma. Neither looked old enough to be driving. Neither looked like murders. They looked like boys. I couldn't help wonder what had happened to them.

Why hadn't someone reached out to them? What had caused someone as young as these two to be so consumed with hate that they had to kill. In such a short amount of time, how had they learned to have such an intense hate? Then I thought of Wayne Pitts. With someone like him influencing their life, learning to hate would have been easy.

"Grandma?"

"Yes Matty."

"Why wasn't someone sent to change the course of their lives?"

"Someone was."

"What happened?"

"They refused help. Those two were conceived in hate. That made reaching them extremely hard. Not impossible. But when a person is conceived in hate, change is something they have to really want. Neither of them wanted to change.

"Neither were willing to put forth the effort. When it was pointed out to them that they were headed for trouble, they responded with a high five."

"But to kill people Grandma?"

"Some people are rude and mean to those around them. Some people burn crosses in the middle of the night. Others kill, Matty."

I looked at the two murders. The youngest one had dirty hair. It was blond, stringy and it came to his shoulders. He was dressed in an old pair of jeans, which were cut off mid thigh. He had on a green tank top and gold canvass Converses. Blondie didn't even have peach fuzz.

Blondie's idiotic friend wore his hair cut short. He wasn't bald like the skinheads of my time but it was buzzed short enough that I could see his scalp. I think he wore it short because of his receding hairline. He was neater than Blondie and probably older by two maybe three years.

He too wore cut off jeans but his had been ironed. His short sleeve red shirt was tucked into his shorts. His Converses were black with high tops. Unlike his partner, he had a nicely trimmed goatee.

"I can't believe we're wasting our time here. Look at all this cheap stuff." Blondie whispered. "This was your pick man."

"I know." Goatee said looking around. "Well, we're here now. Let's see what happens." Blondie shrugged his shoulders and looked around again. He was disgusted by what he saw.

His look of disgust was out of place. While nothing in this kitchen was expensive, everything was clean, well kept and in working order. Just like the car she drove. Most of the things here were probably given to her by well meaning family and friends. Goatee and Blondie knew she had no money. Money wasn't why they'd targeted her in the first place.

Blondie peaked through the doorway that connected the kitchen to the living room. Doorway was really being generous. It was nothing more than a small passage. He stood waiting, listening for any movement or noise that would indicate Bonnie was headed back to the kitchen.

Goatee went to the counter and looked around. He gently touched the counter with two fingers then he brought them to his nose and sniffed them. Apparently satisfied, he bent to sniff the cookies. He stood, looked at the floor, the sink and the stove. Again satisfied, he reached for a cookie.

He took a small bite out of it and chewed slowly, rolling the cookie around in his mouth. After a couple of chews, he popped the rest of the cookie in his mouth. He reached for another. Just as he was about to put that cookie in his mouth, Blondie motioned to him that someone was coming. Rather than put the cookie back, he shoved it in with the first one then he wiped his hands together and waited.

"Hello." Goatee said to Bonnie when she came into the kitchen. Of course, his presence shocked and scared her. She didn't answer him. She simply back peddled.

"Leaving so soon." Blondie said as she backed past him.

He'd been standing against the wall as she walked in. She never saw him until it was too late. Before she could say anything or turn and run, he hit her. Hard!

I reached for her. Blondie's hitting her was so unexpected for both Bonnie and me that both of us were slow to respond. I winced at the sound of her body making contact with the floor. Immediately I dropped to the floor beside her.

She was so still for a moment that I thought she was dead. I checked for a plus. She had one. She was breathing. She lay dazed and confused. But alive.

I backed up until I was as far back as I could go. I looked at the ceiling because I didn't want to look at her. On the ceiling, I saw a heart monitor.

It belonged to Grandma. Only forty-nine beats a minute. Grandma didn't have much longer. Neither did Bonnie.

Movement from Bonnie got my attention. Slowly she sat up. She held her right hand to the right side of her face. Her left hand held her abdomen. Blood trickled from the corner of her mouth.

"For a minute there man, I thought you killed her." Goatee told Blondie.

"I got the touch man. I know just how hard to hit."

"I'm a believer." Goatee said holding his hand up for a high five.

The image of those two laughing and slapping each other five reminded me of what Grandma had said. They had not wanted help. They had been conceived in hate, which made reaching them hard. They were warned.

Grandma's time maybe close. Bonnie's time maybe close. The most important thing was knowing that their time was close too.

"That nigger never knew you were there." Goatee said taking another cookie and popping it in his mouth.

He grabbed another one and handed it to Blondie. Like Goatee he popped the whole thing in his mouth. Then he smiled. I wanted them both to choke.

"Pretty damn good." Blondie said. Goatee nodded then turned to Bonnie.

"Where's the money?"

"My purse." She said then pointed to the chair next to the one I'd been sitting in.

He wiped his hands together then in one step he moved from the counter to the chair. He poured the entire contents of the purse onto the table, shaking it for good measure. Bonnie watched quietly. Her face revealing nothing she felt.

I sat in awe of her. Even with the right side of her face swelling, she was still beautiful. She was calm. And she was handling the situation better than I was. But then I knew more then she did. She was still innocent enough to think money was all they wanted.

"Fifty dollars?" Goatee yelled to Blondie from the table without turning to face him. "Fifty dollars! That's all you got nigger?" He yelled at Bonnie.

"It's all I have. I swear it." Bonnie said obviously wanting them to take the money and go.

I wanted her to scream. I wanted her to at least try and run. She didn't do either. She just sat there. Then I remembered the baby.

While I'd forgot about the baby, I was sure that was all she was thinking about. She felt her best response was to stay calm. To let them have what they wanted so that she could live to see another day and her baby. Damn I hated knowing what I knew.

"Too bad ain't it man?" Goatee asked Blondie. They both laughed and winked at each other. They had known all along she had no money. I was pissed. But that was a feeling I knew well.

"Only for her." Blondie said. "Looks like we'll have to find a way to make this worth our while."

He placed his foot on Bonnie's abdomen then roughly pushed her backwards. She made no sound. She simply closed her eyes. She remained quiet while first Blondie then Goatee took turns raping her.

I crawled out of my corner and headed for the door so that I could leave. I got as far as the door and could go no farther. To keep from watching, I turned to face the corner. I didn't need to see what was going on in order to know what was going on. But I did see it.

As if I had no control of my body, I turned back towards Bonnie. I closed my eyes and turned back to face the corner. I thought about the last time I'd stood in a corner. I must have been about six.

Before traveling very far down memory lane, my body turned back towards Blondie and Goatee. I was going to watch them rape her. Whether I wanted to or not. I didn't want to.

When they were done, Bonnie pulled herself into a fetal position. She cried. Tears rolled from her eyes but she made no noise. It was like she had been struck mute.

Grandma was not mute, however. I could hear her crying even though I couldn't see her. Somehow, I was sure Grandma was crying more for what was to come than for what had just happened. I didn't know what was to come. I just knew whatever they were going to do wasn't going to be good. I knew this because I knew Bonnie was going to die today.

When Goatee and Blondie went back to the table to divide the money, I slid down the wall to the floor. I felt I should go to her. I couldn't. I felt ashamed.

I felt ashamed for a number of reasons. The first of course was because I'd been forced to watch the violation of another person. I was sure I knew what she was feeling. I'd felt it myself.

I felt ashamed because not only had she been violated, they'd also tried to humiliate her. On top of raping her, they'd called her a nigger. They'd laughed at her, hit her. At the moment, I felt ashamed to be a male. White male more to the point.

I was from the nineties. I knew that word was still being used but never by me. I felt no hate towards any one race of people.

I didn't care what color you were. If you were in my way, you were in my way. I was an equal opportunity social train. Get on my tracks and I'll do my best to run you over.

With Blondie and Goatee out of the way, I went to Bonnie. I was a doctor. Despite my knowledge, I knew I would not be able to help her. This thought made me sick.

I knelt at her side anyway. She was trembling, scared and crying. I reached out to stroke her hair with the intentions of…comforting her. I wanted to comfort her.

To my surprise, I was able to do just that. She became tense at first. So did I. But I continued to stroke her hair.

Slowly she started to relax. Soon she all but stopped trembling. She opened her eyes and looked over her shoulder at me. It seemed as though she saw me, actually looked at me. Before I was sure, she closed her eyes again.

I think she saw me! I was sure of it. My shame turned to shock followed by surprise. I was surprised, shocked even happy all at the same time. Then all my feelings gave way to anger. I stood up and turned towards Blondie and Goatee. For the first time since I don't know when, I had a purpose and that purpose was to kick ass.

If they could refuse help, I would refuse to believe I couldn't help. In one step, I was standing behind Goatee. As if he knew I was there, he turned around. I made a fist drew back only to have Goatee walk right through me. I stood shocked and angrier than I've ever been in all my life.

Without turning around, I knew that he went back to the counter to get another cookie. Blondie stayed at the table. He was still turning over the contents of Bonnie's purse trying to determine if there was anything of value there. Both of them were angry now. They'd hoped against hope Bonnie would have more.

I reached out to touch his shoulder. I placed my hand on his shoulder but I couldn't feel him. I had been able to touch Bonnie. At this moment, however, my hand was on Blondie's shoulder but he couldn't feel me and I couldn't feel him.

I reached up to touch his hair. Still I felt nothing. I tried to grab a handful so that I could pull it. My fingers went straight through causing him no discomfort at all.

All of a sudden I was ten years old again. I was sitting in that damn closet doing what I'd been told to do. Listening. Always listening. No matter how hard I prayed I always heard his footsteps approaching.

I stood in Bonnie's kitchen holding my breath. Just like I had held my breath then. I was hoping not this time. I was wishing and praying as I had wished and prayed then that I could hold my breathe long enough to die. I watched a handle, that didn't have a door, turn, much as I'd watched helplessly when I was a child.

I closed my eyes then shook my head. This wasn't real. I wasn't ten any longer. I was twenty-six years old. I was a man. This was not happening.

"No!" I screamed. " I will not let you touch me as an adult like you touched me when I was a child! I'm tired of living in fear! I'm tired of seeing you every time I close my eyes!" I dropped to my knees behind Blondie and started crying.

" I'm just plain tired. I will not let you control me any longer. Go to hell you stupid son of a bitch! I hate you! I hate you!" I stood up screaming.

That little purging of the soul felt good. I might have looked stupid standing and screaming to no one. But it felt good. More to the point I felt good.

"Good for you Matty. Good for you." Grandma said.

"Are we winning Grandma?" I asked wiping away my tears.

"We've made a start. You still have a long road ahead of you and not much time to get to the end of it though."

I looked at Bonnie and dropped to my knees beside her again. I was sorry for what she had gone through. I was sorry for what she was going to go through. I thought about that.

If I was going through what she was going through and there was no way to stop it, what would I want? I'd not want to be alone. Matthew Allen would. Not Matty. Matty would want his tears kissed away.

I had no control over what was happening to Bonnie. However, I could do whatever was possible to let her know she wasn't alone. I have limitations. That was one of the lessons I was meant to learn. I have no choice but to live within them.

But, I also learned that there were ways to go on even with limitations. I realized I didn't have to like my limitations. Just accept them.

I didn't think I could. Not today anyway. I wanted to help. And I was going to find a way to do just that.

When Blondie found nothing of value on the table, he left the kitchen to continue his quest in other parts of the house. Goatee went to the refrigerator; poured himself a glass of milk then had another cookie.

I placed a reassuring hand on Bonnie's shoulder. She looked back at me again then she turned over so that she was facing me and closed her eyes.

"Grandma." I cried. "Please tell me there is something I can do to help."

"You already are child. Can't you see that?"

"But this isn't helping. This isn't enough. I care okay Grandma. I care." I said. "Please tell me how to help her."

"Matty sometimes caring is all one can do." I started to say something else when Blondie came screaming back through the house.

"Nothing! There is absolutely nothing here!" He was fuming. Blondie stepped over Bonnie and me, took the glass of milk from Goatee and drained it in one gulp.

"No nigger should be that pretty." Goatee said studying Bonnie. He had been staring at her while Blondie was gone.

He took a step closer then knelt beside her. Roughly he grabbed her shoulders and pulled her to a sitting position. I placed one arm between him and Bonnie. With the other, I pushed him as hard as I could. I flipped right through him.

"She's too quiet too." Goatee said.

"That's cause she knows her place." Blondie said.

Goatee looked at him seemingly waiting for an explanation. Whatever Blondie had to say, he took his time about it. He stood at the refrigerator; it's door open drinking from a carton of orange juice.

"She found herself a nigger loving white man. Hell she probably loved us."

"Is that right? Too bad he ain't here." Goatee said letting her go. He stood, took a drink from the orange juice carton, swished it around in his mouth then swallowed.

"This was your pick man. I get to pick the next target. Twenty-five dollars. What a waste." Blondie said wiping his mouth.

"Maybe for you but I'm about to get my money's worth." Goatee said winking at Blondie.

I felt like throwing up. I didn't want to go through that again. Then I thought about Bonnie. Neither did she.

I felt nothing. Not this time. I wasn't the one being abused. I knew what she was feeling though. I'd been there and I knew.

Blondie grabbed a hand full of Bonnie's hair and pulled her over. I stood and backed away from them. When I realized where I was, I was standing in the living room.

I'd actually been allowed to leave the kitchen. That meant I didn't have to watch those animals. I turned to leave. Before leaving, I glanced back at Bonnie.

She was staring at me. Her hand reaching out to me. She wanted me to stay with her. How could I say no? I knelt and took her hand in mine. She gripped mine so tight that it hurt. I didn't care about the pain.

The two of them descended upon Bonnie like hungry vultures. All I could do was place my hand over Bonnie's eyes and close my own. I felt her tears as they ran under my fingers. She prayed. I prayed too. It was something I had not done in sixteen years.

"I'm not having as much fun as I should be having." Goatee said.

"It's that damn fat ass stomach of hers." Blondie said.

"I believe you're right." Goatee said as if studying the situation. "Why don't we do something about that?" He said then stood and went to the counter.

There he pulled open a drawer. When he didn't find what he was looking for, he opened another one. Two drawers later, he found what he'd been searching to find. He turned back towards Bonnie.

"What the hell are you doing?" I yelled, stepping into the path of Goatee. Again he walked through me. I might as well have not been there.

What Goatee was holding made Bonnie's eyes open wide. For the first time since she was surprised, Bonnie's face registered fear.

"No. Please don't hurt my baby." Those were the only words Bonnie had saw the need to speak.

"The best nigger is a dead nigger." Goatee said.

At that, Bonnie sat up. She elbowed Blondie in the best place possible. She jumped to her feet and ran for the door. Blondie slumped across the doorway, which hampered her escape.

As she tried to step over him, Goatee grabbed her by her shoulders, pulled her around only to suffer the same fate that Blondie had. Again, Bonnie tried to step over Blondie.

Recovering, he grabbed her by her left foot and tripped her. Bonnie managed to twist sideways so that she could avoid landing on her belly. She screamed.

Her scream was cut off by a hard blow delivered by Blondie to the right side of the head. That stopped her screaming but not her fighting. He pulled her back into the kitchen by her foot and hit her again.

They say nothing hath more fury than a scorned woman. They were wrong. Nothing hath more fury than a woman trying to protect her child.

Bonnie punched Blondie back causing his nose to bleed. By the sound coming from her hand, she did more damage to herself than to him. That didn't stop her. Had there only been one of them, she would have won. I have no doubt of that. But there were two.

Goatee finished what Blondie started. The second punch to her face knocked her unconscious. When all the commotion was over, I realized that someone was screaming. Since Bonnie was unconscious, that someone had to be me.

Thank God she was unconscious! I wished I were. I also wished that she'd stay unconscious. She didn't.

She was awakened by the pain the knife caused cutting through her skin, her muscles and into her abdomen then her womb. I tried to get to her but Blondie held her hands over her head. Goatee was leaning over her abdomen as he worked. My punches had no effect. My pushing didn't move them.

To prevent her from screaming, Blondie stuffed Bonnie's mouth with a dishcloth. Eventually weakness and delirium did a better job at muffling her screams than any cloth ever could. My screams continued as strong as ever though.

I screamed for her as well as for myself. It was all I could do. Grandma promised I wouldn't lose my mind. I was sure I would anyway.

In the beginning, Bonnie had struggled against Blondie's hold. Like her screams, her struggling weakened then stopped altogether. Not that it mattered. Her struggles were no more effective than her screams had been.

When the baby was exposed, I knelt opposite of Goatee and tried to push him back in. He was not ready to be born. It was not time for him to be in this hostile world.

My hands became warm and wet from my efforts. Bonnie's blood was now on my hands. But for a totally different reason from the one that put her blood on their hands. But that was all I got for my efforts. I was unable to keep the baby from being delivered prematurely. When Bonnie saw her baby, she focused her eyes and reached for him.

The baby gasped for air. His little body was shocked by the abrupt delivery as well as by the cold air that surrounded him, invading the warmth he had once known. He! A son. Bonnie had given birth to a son.

The little boy gasped again then cried a pitifully weak cry. Bonnie's hands shook slightly as she held them out, waiting for her baby to be placed in them. Her little boy gasped for air and cried again. Then seeming to realize something was wrong, he reserved his strength by not trying to cry. He simply concentrated on breathing.

Blondie and Goatee laughed at Bonnie's pleas for her baby. They were both spiteful and cruel. Goatee would place the baby within Bonnie's reach then pull him away just as she had her hand on him. I tried to take the baby from Goatee.

When I couldn't, I pushed his arms down hoping Bonnie could get a better grip on her son. Nothing worked. Knowing I couldn't touch Goatee, I blew as hard as I could into his eyes. This made him blink or maybe he blinked on his own. Either way it did nothing to make him release the baby.

"Let go you stupid son of a bitch." I hissed through clenched teeth. "Can't you see he'll die if you don't let him go?"

"My baby. Please give me my baby." She whispered. Barely able to get the words out.

She was slowly dying. As slow as her son was. That revelation packed one hell of a punch. I didn't know the baby died with her. Grandma hadn't told me that.

Or did he? Maybe he doesn't die. I jumped to my feet and ran for the door hoping to find a phone. There wasn't one in the kitchen. The door was as far as I could go. The baby was going to die. He had died that day along with his mother twenty-five years ago.

Thirty-nine beats per minute. I counted as Grandma's heart beat sounded in my ears. Didn't I have enough to worry about without knowing how little time Grandma had left too? When I didn't think things could get any worse, I was proven wrong.

"How long do you think he'll live?" Blondie asked taking the baby from Goatee. He gave the baby to Bonnie. She held him close to her. She tried to keep him warm. She tried to console him.

Initially, I thought giving the baby to Bonnie was an act of kindness on Blondie's part. Nothing could have been farther from the truth. Blondie had a more sinister goal in mind. He knew that Bonnie would do anything to get to her baby. He wanted to see just what anything meant.

While Goatee pondered the question, I turned my attentions back to Bonnie and her baby. I watched as she kissed her struggling son's head with trembling, knowing yet loving lips. I watched her and everything she did.

So did the two of them. By now, Bonnie didn't look black any more. Her light skin had become very pale as her life slowly ebbed from her body. Her lips were now blue. A sign that she wasn't getting enough oxygen.

Her hands reminded me of my mother's. They were bony, white, cold. She was now gasping for air much like her baby boy was doing. The lost of blood was making it impossible for her to breathe. Immature lungs were making it impossible for her son to breathe.

"Five minutes." Goatee said.

"No way. He won't last that long."

"Bet."

"I bet" Blondie said. "And while we're at it, I bet if I put him over here." Blondie said taking the little boy from Bonnie. "She won't get to him before he dies."

"Don't do this." I croaked. My voice was hoarse, my nose congested. I didn't recognize my own voice. It didn't matter. No one heard me.

"You're on." Goatee said.

Blondie took the baby. He laid him on the floor in front of the refrigerator. The length was no more than two maybe three steps away. For Bonnie, who was weak, in pain and basically just dying, it was a hell of a long two, maybe three steps. But she was willing to make the trip.

With energy that she should not have had, she pulled herself to all fours. When she did, an ungodly amount of blood spilled from her open womb. Her intestines dragged the floor. None of that mattered to her. Nothing was going to stop her.

With strength only a mother could possess, she started across the floor to her baby boy. He gasped. She gasped. Breathing was becoming less frequent for him. Breathing was becoming less frequent for her as well.

When I saw how determined she was, I went to her little boy and knelt beside him. I was determined she would have a prize at the end of her labored journey. While Goatee held his watch, Blondie looked on. I preformed rescue breathing on Bonnie's little boy. In between breaths, I looked to see how close she was. To my shock and surprise her eyes locked with mine.

When she finally arrived, she smiled at me. I couldn't believe it. "Thank you Jesus." She said.

"Jesus? No, not me." I whispered.

"Angel?" She asked.

"I've never been called that either."

"You were sent to help me?" She asked. She was out of breath when she finished.

"Yes." I answered.

"Angel." She said then smiled. So did I.

Her smile was wondrous. I remembered how my mother had looked when she smiled at Chris. It had been just as wonderful and she had been dying too.

After thanking me, Bonnie laid beside her son. She attempted to pull her son to her. By now, she was far too weak. If the baby had been another step farther, I'm not sure she would have…yes she would have. She would have reached him no matter how far away he was. That I was sure of.

Bonnie slid her hands under him trying again to lift him. I placed my hands under hers. Together we lifted him. She then pulled her arms back and nestled the baby against her chest. With the gapping wound that was now her abdomen, this nestling actually made it look as though she was trying to put him back inside of her.

"Thank you so much." She whispered barely audible even to me.

She found the strength to kiss her son once more. Then she died. Less than a minute later, her son took his last breath.

Thank God! After all she'd been through, she didn't have to watch him die too. I sat with my back against the wall and I cried. She had called me an angel. She had thanked me. I had been there when she needed someone and she had thought I was an angel.

I was warm and cold all over. I was happy and sad. Feelings I couldn't ever remember having were all happening at once. I was confused and more alive than I'd ever been before.

I'd just experienced something I never wanted to ever experience again. But I wouldn't give up the experience for all the money in the world. I kept playing the events over and over again.

She called me an angel. Someone thought I was an angel. What I was feeling is what it must feel like to give birth. What I was feeling was the greatest yet the most painful moment of my life. I was alive!

"Four minutes fifty seconds. You lose." Blondie said.

"Yeah well, she made it to the baby before he died so it's a draw."

Grandma was right. These two were despicable. The only consolation I had was knowing that they were both going to pay for what they had done.

"So much for that. What say we get cleaned up? Blow this lousy twenty-five dollars and move on. Who knows when hubby will come home?"

"Cool by me." Goatee said bending over Bonnie and her son. "Hey did you see this?" He pulled on a chain that hung around Bonnie's neck.

I looked too. The chain was gold. Nothing fancy but the charm attached to it appeared to be.

It depicted a mother holding her newborn baby. I looked back at Bonnie. She had looked much like that mother for a short time. The mother on the pendant had a halo around her head. I guess now, so did Bonnie.

I'd never seen a pendant like it before. It was oval in shape and it appeared to be made of either black pearl or black opal. Goatee took the necklace off, went to the sink, washed the blood off it and his hands.

"Think it's worth anything?"

"The gold probably is but I don't know about that." Blondie said pointing to the pendant.

Goatee put the necklace on. It fit snuggly around his neck, which made the pendant sit right in the center of his neck, right below his Adams apple.

I stood and walked closer. I knew, without knowing how I knew, that the necklace was very valuable. Without thinking, I grabbed for it. The necklace pulled tightly around Goatee's neck. He reached up and grabbed for whatever it might have been hung on while coughing and turning red.

"What's the matter man?"

"I must have this damn thing hooked on something. It's choking me."

I pulled tighter. I had wanted them to choke earlier, now at least one of them would. I was just about to yank it off his neck when something told me not to. It took everything I had but I finally let the necklace go.

"I don't see nothing man." Blondie said.

"It's lose now. Look at my neck. Ain't it red? It was hooked on something."

"Yeah man. Must have got hooked on this tag back here. You want me to pull it off.

"Nah. I'll be ditching these clothes anyway."

I don't know why it was important to let Goatee have the necklace. But everything in my gut told me that the necklace was valuable in more ways than I had been privileged to know.

"Hey are you sure you didn't miss anything? I mean I don't see no wedding ring on her finger. We know she's married. Don't we?" Goatee said patting Blondie on the shoulder as he passed him.

"Hey I hadn't thought about that." Blondie said following Goatee out of the kitchen. After a thorough search that led to them ransacking a once perfectly organized and happy home, a metaphor that did not escape me, the two of then failed to turn up the ring.

"Forget the ring. We need to get moving. By the looks of things it's probably cheap." Goatee said.

"Flip you for the master bath." Blondie said undaunted by their failure. "Heads." The coin landed with the tails side up. "Fuck it!" He said already headed for the hall bathroom. His shirt off, his pants already unzipped.

Goatee stood watching him and laughing. After Blondie disappeared, he looked at his hands, which were still streaked with blood. Then he looked at his clothes. Since he did the cutting, his clothes were saturated with Bonnie's blood. Specks of blood also peppered his arms and his face. As he looked at himself, disgust crossed his face. He too started striping in the hall.

I went back to the living room. There, I sat on the floor and waited. The sofa and chair had been overturned out of fun more than as part of the actual search. I wanted to go outside but was not allowed to do so.

I felt sick. I wondered what would happen if I vomited. At the rate things were going if I didn't get out of here soon, I'd find out sooner rather than later. The smell of all that blood was making my stomach lurch. It was a smell that permeated the air throughout the whole house.

The smell soaked the hairs in my nose. It ran down my throat each time I swallowed. It bathed my skin and it turned on a button in my brain that guaranteed I'd never forget the smell of blood for as long as I lived. My only consolation was that it was no longer on my hands.

I needed to shower too but not here. The bathrooms, here or anywhere for that matter, weren't big enough for the kind of shower I needed. The only place big enough was one of the four oceans. For I was certain that only a body of water as big as the ocean, could adequately scrub the smell of Bonnie's blood from every pore of my body, my mind, my soul.

While sitting and pondering the events that I'd experience today, new feelings raged through me and I felt a profound sorrow for the two lives lost. It soon dawned on me that neither of the showers were running. I walked to the hall bathroom. Blondie was no longer there. His blood soaked clothes were.

They lay waiting to be discovered or picked up. But certainly not put back on. I moved to the master bedroom. Both Blondie and Goatee were standing before a mirror already dressed.

I'd wondered what they would do for clothes. I wondered no more. With the help of Lawrence's clothes, the two of them would soon leave pretty much as they had come. The difference now, their clothes are a little baggy. That's because Lawrence is bigger than either of them. Another difference, they were both bare footed. Neither of which would draw much attention this hot July day.

Once they were both dressed, Goatee searched for something to write with. He found a marker in the nightstand. With it, he wrote the message, which had invoked fear for many people over the last few months. It was the same message that would inform local officials that this was only one case out of many. He wrote.

"I just rid the world of two more niggers." He then gave the marker to Blondie who went to write the same thing on the mirror in the hall bathroom.

BLINK! I found myself sitting in the backseat of the stolen Cadillac. Neither of them had been willing to give up the nice cool ride of the Cadillac for the bucket of bolts Bonnie had been driving. On the seat beside me, sat a bag with their bloody clothes in it. A dumb move on their part but I hoped a dumb move in our favor.

As before, I wasn't sure when we left the house or what direction we were headed in. I wasn't sure when they'd bagged their clothes or put them in the car. I wasn't even sure when we got in the car or what street we were on. The only thing I was sure of was that I was no longer at Bonnie's house. For that I was thankful.

I knew, however, that I would be back and that made me think of Lawrence. He was going to be devastated. I wondered what I would do if I were him. I had no experience to base my answer on but I was sure, without a shadow of a doubt, that I would kill them both.

If I were him, I would kill them without regards to my safety or future. I would kill them without fear of being caught or prosecuted to the full extent of the law. I would kill them without fear of anything because there would be nothing left to fear. Everything I have is already gone. Therefore I would have nothing to lose.

For the first time in my life, I looked forward to the kind of love Bonnie and Lawrence shared together. I looked forward to being a father. I couldn't wait to line my family up so that I could kiss away their tears when needed. That was a strange thought but for the first time I realized that being able to comfort someone was vital. Not just to the person being comforted but to the person doing the comforting.

"How bout that Grandma. I'm looking forward to comforting someone again!"

"How bout that indeed Matty." Grandma said as pleased with me as I was with myself. Then she said something that surprised me. "Ready to come home Matty?"

"Come home? Do I have a choice?"

"Yes you do."

"Then if it's alright with you, I'd like to see this thing through."

"Guess what Matty?"

"What Grandma?"

"We're winning!" At that I smiled. Not for long though. Grandma had a coughing fit and I realized that her heart rate was only thirty-seven beeps per minutes.

"Grandma are you alright?" I asked but got no answer.

"How much gas we got?" Goatee asked bringing me back to the past.

"Quarter tank. There's a Fast Fare around here somewhere. I saw it earlier. I thought I'd stop there, fill up and see if we could add to our stash. Twenty-five dollars ain't gonna get us far."

"Let's do it then." Goatee said turning his attention to the street.

Oh no, I thought. First Bonnie and her baby, now Grace. These two were a non-stop destruct-o team.

"There it is!" Goatee yelled and pointed, having spotted the convenience store first. I knew these two were caught but at what point and how many lives were lost before they were, I wondered.

"Don't answer that Grandma!" I said. I wanted to know but I didn't want to bother Grandma for the answer. In fact, all I wanted was for her to rest. Her time was shorter than ever. As her doctor, I ordered rest. Then a thought occurred to me.

By asking to stay in the past, would I ever see her alive in the present. I knew her heart rate was weak and so was she. I opened my mouth to call her name but didn't. She'd said we were winning. She had been happy that I wanted to stay. Since we were winning, I thought it best to leave well enough alone.

"Please be alive when I get back Grandma." I quietly prayed. Then I focused my attention back on the situation at hand.

I sat in the car and waited. Blondie and Goatee got out to look around. I would take my place, wherever that place was, when the time came. This no longer bothered me. I hoped very little would, from now on out.

BLINK! My place was inside the store with Grace, who was behind the counter. From there, I watched Blondie and Goatee looking around. To Grace, they were two kids goofing off while they gassed up. I knew better. They were casing the place trying to make sure they were alone. They were.

I stood behind the counter and watched Grace work. She stamped prices on cartons of cigarettes then stacked them to the side so that she could later log them in. Somehow, I knew she was to price and stock as many of those cigarettes as she could in as little time as possible.

This worried me. I feared she would not pay enough attention to her next customers. In this case, that could cost her, her life. Nervously I watched and waited.

It was in that watchful state that I discovered why Bonnie had checked on Grace. I hadn't paid her much attention earlier but then she really hadn't given me a reason to. Now I had one. Earlier Grace had worn a jacket. In the absence of company, she sported short sleeves. On the back of her left arm were four small purple marks. Bruises!

She had been grabbed...hard. I knew Grace had been lying earlier. Here was the proof. Grace hadn't returned Bonnie's phone calls because she hadn't been in town. She had been with him and he had hurt her once again. It became clear to me that Grace wasn't just a member of The Walking Wounded Club. She was the president.

I should have known better. However, I was unable to stop myself. Gently, I touched the larger of the bruises. My touch caused Grace to jump, which of course caused me to jump. I was still having a hard time determining what I could do and what I couldn't. Touching Grace was something I could do but should not have.

Unwittingly, I scared her, which caused her to drop her jacket. When she did, she quickly turned to face me. When she saw no one, she looked to her left then to her right. Still not finding the offender, she turned all the way around until she was back to her starting position.

Suspicious but now convinced she was alone, Grace grabbed her jacket and put it on before Blondie pushed the door open. As much as I'd wanted to, I'd not been seen. I opened my mouth again to ask Grandma a question but didn't.

All of this took place twenty-five years ago. As hard as it was to comprehend and accept, all I could do was watch.

"Hi. How you guys doing?"

I looked at Grace's face. I looked past the bruises, past the abuse and saw a woman who was happier than she'd been in days. Her happiness was made possible because Bonnie had stopped by earlier. Earlier Grace had looked tired, whipped if you will. Now she looked like a flower waiting to bloom.

Her smile spread from her lips to her eyes. There, a small fire burned. I got the same impression now that I got earlier. All she needed was a little TLC. Just a little and she could be persuaded to come fully alive.

"How you doing ma'am?" Goatee asked. "We're gonna get some other stuff to go along with the gas."

"That'll be fine." She said.

Goatee nodded then headed for the back of the store where all the beverages were. There, he studied the selections while Blondie went to the chip and dip aisles. He hadn't eaten as many cookies and he was hungry.

Opening a bag of Lay's potato chips, he stuffed a hand full of them in his mouth before grabbing up a family size bag of Ruffles. He then grabbed two cans of onion dip and started for the counter. Once there, he smiled at Grace and unloaded his arms.

"I'll bring the empty bag back so you can ring it up with all the other stuff." He said. She nodded but continued pricing and stacking. "Oh, can you add a carton of those Marlboro's you got stacked there to the pile please?" He asked pointing to a stack of cartons that hadn't been priced yet.

"Those haven't been logged in yet." Grace said reaching for a carton over her head. She placed it with the pile of junk food.

"Logged in?"

"FDA requirement. I'm not sure why." She said laughing. "I guess it's their way of tracking the cigarettes in case there's a bad batch."

"Really?" He asked surprised. Twenty-five years ago the hazards of smoking hadn't been thoroughly pressed upon the public. "So how will they know I bought this carton?"

"I don't know." She said shrugging her shoulders. "All I was told is that it's a FDA requirement. Quite frankly, I think it has more to do with billing than anything else. I log in how many and what brand we received and they compare it to their records so that we can pay the company."

"Oh." He said and turned to shop some more.

Grace was just about to go back to pricing but stopped. For the longest time, she stood staring at him as he walked away. I cleared my throat hoping to get her attention. I didn't want either of them to look up and notice that she was staring. When she continued to stare, I stepped behind her and touched her arm.

She hadn't heard me clearing my throat but she was able to still feel my touch. This time my touch didn't scare her. She was too numb for that. My touch simply caused her to turn away from Blondie and Goatee.

With her back turned to them, she held her right hand in front of her and looked at the palm of it. She brought that same hand up to her face and turned it from front to back over and over. It looked to me as if she was trying to find something she'd lost. Not only did she seemed to be looking for something that was lost, she seemed to be lost.

I looked to see what Blondie and Goatee were doing. They were unaware of Grace's bizarre behavior. Noticing that Grace was too busy to watch both of them, Goatee slipped into the back room.

"Come on Grace snap out of it." When she didn't respond, I touched her shoulder.

This time my touch caused her eyes to focus. She turned to face Blondie and Goatee only to find Goatee was no where to be found. While she waited, she absent mindedly picked up a carton of cigarettes and flipped them over and over until she saw Goatee coming from the direction of the bathroom.

Blondie approached him. From where we were standing, it looked like they were consulting each other about the band of beer Blondie was holding. Instead, Goatee was filling him in on what he'd found. They were alone. There was a safe in the back office. It was locked but easy enough to open.

While they were talking, Grace did something that surprised the hell out of me. She pushed the silent alarm.

"That a girl Grace! Now make their job harder. Make them think twice before attacking you. Move your butt from behind this counter."

I don't think Grace's next response was because of anything I'd said. She hadn't been able to hear me up to this point. I think she responded because she had a strong desire to help catch these two or a strong desire to live. Maybe it was both. Either way, she moved from behind the counter and went to stand by a magazine rack, which was by the door.

There she lost focus again. She went back to looking at her hand. Again, turning it over and over.

"What are you looking for Grace?" I asked.

Of course, she didn't answer me. I moved close enough to her so that I could see her hand. The hand was dirty from opening and lifting boxes but there was nothing else to see.

"There's nothing there Grace." When she didn't stop, I stepped back. "Okay Matty she's in shock." I told myself. "Just give her a little time. In the meantime, keep an eye on those two. If they try anything, get her attention by touching her. Assuming you'll be able to if you need to." I stopped and took a deep breath.

I realized I was speaking out loud. Out of habit, I looked around. "Just remember you're not losing your mind Matty. Grandma assured you, your sanity would not be at risk." I told myself.

I knew I was just responding to the situation. Nothing more. I trusted Grandma. Besides talking out loud seemed to make it easier for me to think. All that mattered right now was trying to keep Grace safe.

Once again, I looked to see what Blondie and Goatee were doing. They were watching Grace and they were pissed. Good! Her being at the door was slowing up their plans. I liked it.

BLINK! All right! Grandma was Back! I knew this because out of the blue I knew why Grace was staring at her hand.

When Bonnie was in earlier, Grace used that hand to feel the baby kicking. Now she knew that kick was the closest she'd ever come to touching or holding that baby. In fact, she knew, without knowing how she knew for sure, that, that morning was the last time she'd ever see Bonnie alive.

I wasn't sure how she knew either. All I knew was that she considered Bonnie to be her best friend. In fact, I remember her telling Bonnie "you are so young so sweet and innocent. I hope you are always like that and that you never have anything happen to you that will change you."

When Grace made that wish, she'd meant it. Now she somehow knew Bonnie had experienced something for worse than loss of innocence.

Now that I knew what was going on with Grace, I wondered how she knew. What had given these two away? Not that I cared. I wanted them to be caught but there was truly nothing about them that would have made me raise an eyebrow.

The only things different about them were their clothes. Surely that couldn't be it. It wasn't the necklace. Goatee hasn't been close enough for Grace to see it yet. All that was left were the clothes.

I believed both Goatee and Blondie to be stupid but neither had been stupid enough to wear anything with Lawrence's name on it. This is a small town, I reminded myself. Anything was possible. Even knowing your neighbor's clothes.

I wanted to believe that was impossible. Yet, stranger things have happened. My being twenty-five years in the past was proof of that. Lately, I was starting to believe nothing was impossible.

"You two let me know when you're ready." Grace said. She never turned away from the window.

Thank God. Grace was back. I ran my hand through my hair and stepped back. For the moment she didn't need me.

"She just needed time Matty. She knew she'd do Bonnie, the baby or herself no good if she was dead by the time the police arrived."

Grandma sounded awful. She sounded as if she'd just run a race. She was panting hard. Every once in a while, I heard her wheezing. Grandma didn't have asthma. Her distress was coming from all the fluid gathering in her lungs.

"Grandma I ordered you to rest didn't I?" I tried to sound angry but if the truth were told I was glad to hear her voice. It meant she was still alive.

I was more worried about her now than ever. I wished I'd gone back when I had the chance. I even thought about asking her if she would bring me back now. It's just that she'd been so happy when I asked to stay. I wish I knew what to do.

She was weak. I knew that for a fact because it had taken her three times as long to reveal to me what was wrong with Grace.

"I'm okay Matty. Don't worry about me."

"Grandma you can barely breathe. How can I not worry about you? That is why you sent me here isn't it?"

"Yes. But your job is not done there."

"It's not?" I asked but she didn't answer. "Will I ever see you again Grandma?"

"I don't know child." She said then she was gone.

Now I really wanted to leave. Grandma knew everything. I knew I couldn't though. I didn't know what else was expected of me here but if this is where I am supposed to be; here is where I'll stay. I owed that much to Grandma and to myself.

I leaned against the door and watched Grace as she worked. For the first time in my life, I felt a peace I've never known before. Even though the two murders haven't been caught, I knew Grace was safe. I also knew they would soon be caught.

Grace's position at the magazine rack was perfect. From there, she was safe. From there, she could watch the road, the store and them. From there, she could give the illusion of working while really reflecting on her life. So could I. Neither of us liked what we saw. Both of us were getting better though.

Two and a half minutes after pushing the silent alarm, Grace wiped her hands together and walked back to the counter. She picked up a pad and checked two items off. From where Blondie and Goatee were standing, it looked as if she'd accomplished two tasks and was now happily crossing them off her list. From where I was standing, I saw two check marks on a blank sheet of paper. When she was done, she laid the pad face down then went back to pricing cigarettes.

Blondie and Goatee decided enough time had been lost. They approached Grace ready to end this little visit. By the time they noticed the police car, it was stopping in front of the store. They looked at each other and ever so slightly nodded. Grace didn't notice.

I noticed. Then I wondered what had brought these two together. Did they grow up in the same neighborhood, did they meet at some reform school or were they cellmates in some state pin? I know they've been headed for trouble for a while now because Grandma told me they'd been warned.

I knew they weren't brothers. Not blood brothers anyway. Yet, they were as close if not closer than most brothers were. I figured a lot of that came from all the time they've spent together and all the secrets they've shared. But there was something else. It was almost as if they could read each other's thoughts. It was that or they've planned for every worse case scenario they may have to face.

Case in point was the nod that they'd just shared. It was just a nod to me but I knew for them, I was sure Grandma was the reason for my privileged information, that nod meant time to go. Tally what you have its check out time. I knew they both hoped this was just a routine patrol and that the officer wouldn't come in. Just to be on the safe side, they slowly put back what they were holding.

Outside, the officer assessed the situation without seeming to. He saw two kids. He saw that Grace was okay or at least she looked to be okay. Unsure, he wrote a couple of questions on a small piece of paper then put it in his front pocket with some change. If he couldn't figure out what was wrong then he'd ask her what was wrong by paying for something.

Slowly he got out. Thank God he was one of the good guys. He was big. Big Red as a matter of fact. So far, however, Big Red was unimpressed by the call to drop everything and come running. As bad as I wanted him to, he didn't come right in. He continued to look like he was busy with his patrol.

"I think this'll do it for us ma'am." Goatee said.

This was the first time Goatee and Grace had been face to face. It goes without saying that she didn't miss seeing the necklace. At the sight of it, her mouth fell open. That got the Big Red's attention. For the first time since pulling to a stop in front of the store, he looked directly into the store.

Grace's recovery was remarkable. She placed her hand over her mouth, closed her eyes and sneezed and sneezed and sneezed. Tears watered her eyes then ran down her face. She turned her back to Blondie and Goatee, grabbed some tissue and sneezed some more. She was shaking now. The sneezes help to hide that fact. Big Red didn't know what was going on but he knew it was time to go in.

His opening the door drew Blondie and Goatee's attention from Grace. This distraction bought Grace some time and Big Red's presence helped her compose herself. She turned around so that she could help finish what she had started.

"Sorry gentlemen." Grace said, tears still in her eyes. "It must be something you're wearing." Pun intended. "I have allergies something awful."

I knew Grace's comment had a double meaning. What I didn't know is if Big Red knew. I watched him watching Grace. His expression was blank. Blondie and Goatee definitely didn't get the message. Instead of understanding, they thought her allergies were real and they both took a step backwards apologizing to her.

"Howdy Grace. You haven't been to see Dr. Banks yet have you?" Big Red asked standing in the doorway.

That name fit him to a tee. He was a big man. When I say big, I don't mean fat. Big Red stands at six feet seven inches and he weights two hundred and eighty pounds. All muscle. A man of that size should not be allowed to carry a gun unless he is capable of smiling. At the moment, he was doing just that.

Based on his size, I expected his voice to vibrate off all the walls. It didn't. When he spoke to Grace, his voice was gentle, caring even loving. That last part was something Blondie, Goatee and I picked up on, not Grace.

"Boys." Big Red said. They both nodded a hello to him but didn't speak. Instead, they turned back to Grace. That wanted to get out in a bad way.

"Howdy yourself Big Red. I'll be right with you." She told him then she turned back to Blondie and Goatee. "You guys can come closer. My nose is stopped up now. I can't smell a thing." She took their items and started arranging them on the counter.

"Big Red I've been meaning to call you and get directions to Dr Banks office." She said but didn't look at him. "I go by over that way all the time but being new I'm not sure which office he's in. Isn't he in the building behind that furniture store? That place is called the pocket isn't it?"

"That's right." Big Red said puzzled as hell but not showing it.

"Is his office on the left side?"

"That's him. He's been expecting you. I told him you were having trouble breathing all this fresh air." She smiled.

"You two having a party? Look at all this junk! Don't you know this stuff is no good for you? It'll rot your teeth right out your head." Blondie and Goatee just laughed.

Without warning, Blondie made a fist. That told Goatee they didn't have enough money. While still laughing, Goatee tilted his head forward. Without using his mouth, Goatee said, 'man this could get messy.'

They were going to have to put a lot of stuff back. Neither were willing to bring out the ill-gotten gains of their latest caper. They couldn't. They had to wash the money because of all the blood. Neither wanted to explain wet money in dry pockets.

"That'll be forty-two dollars and fifty- two cents." Grace said.

Without the fifty dollars from Bonnie, Blondie and Goatee were short twelve dollars. They looked at the items on the counter trying to decide what to put back while deciding what to keep. At the moment, they felt being embarrassed was all they had to worry about. Neither of them suspected Big Red was actually there because he'd been called. I know because they already winked at each other. That wink said Big Red was here to see Grace personally.

"You boys aren't from around here are you?" Big Red asked as they grabbed a hand full of junk and turned to replace it. His voice was somewhat deeper and not as friendly as before.

"No sir." Goatee said. "We're just passing through."

"Where you from?"

"Atlanta."

While Big Red was occupying Blondie and Goatee, Grace looked for something to sit on. All of a sudden her legs got weak and she felt as if she'd fall. She didn't want that to happen. She wasn't ready to totally let her guard down. Not until those two were behind bars. When she couldn't find anything that would hold her weight, she leaned against the counter.

She was tired. She was hurting. Her mental anguish was as bad as any physical pain she'd endured recently. Her best friend was gone. With that thought, she looked at Blondie and Goatee. They were the reason for her pain yet they'd never laid a hand on her. They were also the reason for her future loneliness.

Grace remembered a time when all she wanted was to be alone. Bonnie would hear none of that. Bonnie had been like a ray of sunlight in her life. She seemed to know when Grace's reasons for getting out of bed were low. She seemed to know when Grace was hurting more than usual. She remembered special days with cookies, cards, phone calls or a quick visit. These two had taken all that away and so much more.

I looked from Grace to Big Red. He reminded me of Paul Bunyan. Give him an axe and a big blue ox and he'd look just like him. Big Red was Chief John Boatwright's nickname. No one who knew him ever called him John though.

Big Red didn't come in to the store. He simply stood in the doorway looking for the clue he'd been given or maybe he was blocking the door. I wasn't sure which. Maybe it was both. It wasn't until Blondie turned his back to him that he found what he was looking for. It was at that point that I decided he was definitely blocking the door.

I walked behind Blondie and looked at his back. I saw nothing on him that would give me a reason to call the police. I looked back at Grace then Big Red. Whatever it was they saw caused Big Red to be more than red. He was a shade of purple.

"You want coffee Big Red?" Grace asked getting his attention. That was her way of letting him know she had more to tell him.

"You got a fresh pot ready?" He asked looking at her. So did Blondie and Goatee.

"No. But it won't take me but a minute."

"I got a minute." He said.

"How bout you two? Want a cup of coffee?"

"No ma'am."

Big Red didn't have to go anywhere and with him standing in the doorway these two weren't going anywhere either. No one would go anywhere until he found out why Grace had called him. With the two of them now occupied, Grace told Big Red what she wanted him to know. She placed her cross pendant in her hand then ran her flat hand over her hair.

That was more information than he could handle. He shook his head and looked to heaven. I knew what that sign meant.

I looked at Blondie's back again. Nothing. I don't know how but somehow it seemed as if Grace knew these two were wearing Lawrence's' clothes. Big Red seemed to know it too. Goatee having Bonnie's necklace on meant something very bad had happened to her. Murder ranked high on their list.

Big Red was no longer smiling. He was trying desperately not to lose control. He needed to think.

By now Blondie and Goatee were a little suspicious. The fact that this big man was still standing in the door fueled that suspicion. Goatee looked at Grace. It was then that his suspicions were confirmed but for the wrong reasons. He passed his money to Blondie. That meant they'd been targeted as shoplifters.

That was okay with them. Neither had stolen anything. This little hick town chief would make a mistake; feel bad about it then let them go. They would still be long gone by the time hubby called about their true crime.

"Is there a problem boys?" Big Red asked.

This little game he was playing with them would have been fun had the stakes not been so high. Big Red was an outdoorsman. That was really the biggest reason for his name. His complexion was red due to all the sun he gets from being outside.

His favorite sport is fishing. In fact, he has told many people that when he wasn't fishing, he was still fishing. 'That's all police work is really. You put the bait on the hook then sit back and wait for a bite. The worse the crime, the harder and longer it takes to reel em in.'

"Can't seem to count today." Goatee answered.

"Maybe that's cause you weren't planning on paying." Big Red said smiling again.

"We've got money officer." Blondie said turning to face Big Red. The challenge made the hair on the back of his neck stand up.

"With both of us grabbing stuff, we just grabbed too much. That's all." Goatee said. He wanted to defuse the situation. This was not a good time for a confrontation.

Generally, when the two of them were facing a situation similar to this one, Blondie's big mouth and short fuse worked in their favor. Something about Big Red, however, told Goatee it would not work today. In fact, Blondie's big mouth just might get them hurt, detained even arrested. None of which would be good for them. To change the general plan, he looked at his watch hoping only Blondie would notice.

"Listen to your buddy." Big Red said.

Neither could resist looking at each other. Goatee had been very subtle. The signal was a common movement. One I've done a hundred times tonight myself. But Big Red had been watching them and learning.

"Look, gas is the only thing we can't return. Why don't we just pay for that and leave. We haven't done anything wrong." Goatee reasoned.

"What's the problem here anyway?" Blondie asked.

"I think the problem is you boy."

"Hey man; just give her five dollars so we can get out of here." Blondie told Goatee then started walking for the door.

Big Red, who had been leaning against the door jam, stood his full six feet seven inches. This seemed to cause the door to practically disappear. Big Red made it clear to Blondie that he was going to have to go through him. Something Blondie decided he wasn't quite ready to do.

"Grace call Bonnie's house for me. See if she answers." Grace looked at Big Red. She knew Bonnie wouldn't answer. "We have to make sure." At that Grace nodded. Big Red turned back to Blondie and Goatee.

"You boys got that routine down to a tee don't you?" He smiled again. When neither of them answered, Big Red addressed them again. "That's okay. I've got a few routines of my own."

I knew the minute I saw Big Red I would like him and I did. I couldn't wait to meet him. He looked like a kick ass kind of guy and now he sounded like one. I felt safe and I wasn't even in danger. What puzzled me was why was he here?

"Are you holding us for some reason?" Goatee asked.

"As a matter of fact, I am. I'm just trying to figure out how many reasons I'm going to hold you for and just how serious those reasons are. Plans to rob this store will probably be the least of the charges."

"Hey man..." Blondie started to say.

"Big Red there's no answer."

"Call the station for me would ya Grace? Have Ron run over to the Phillips house and check on her. Have him call Johnny Stevens. Tell him to take Johnny along with him. Tell him to call him over the phone. I don't want any radios used. Got that?" Grace nodded and dialed the phone.

"Oh Grace." Big Red said after a moment's hesitation. "Tell Ron to turn off his radio. Tell him to pass the word on. I want no radios on. Then tell Jennifer to call all deputies in. I want all available officers called in." Grace nodded again then started speaking into the phone.

"Hey man I don't know what this is all about. You can't prove nothing." Blondie yelled.

"I can prove those aren't your clothes boy. Right now that's all I need to prove. But that's not all that I can prove."

"You're out of your mind. These are our clothes." Blondie said.

"Liar!" Grace yelled. She was standing at the counter the orders from Big Red carried out. "Those are Lawrence Phillips clothes."

"You people are nuts." Blondie said.

"I'd watch my mouth if I were you boy."

"Listen officer, there's been some kind of mistake here. We don't know any Lawrence Phillips. All we want to do is pay for our gas and leave." Goatee said. At that, he placed five dollars on the counter and turned to face Big Red.

Big Red hadn't moved. He'd rushed over prepared to find shoplifters. He was prepared to defend Grace if it came to that. After figuring out Grace's gesture, he even thought he was prepared to see the evidence. He was not.

Seeing that necklace around Goatee's neck did something to him. What he felt was beyond plain anger. It was beyond shock. For the first time since coming to this town, he felt like he was in the rat race of old. He, like Grace, knew that if Goatee had that necklace on, there was nothing he could do. What had happened had already happened. All that was left was to make sure justice was served.

Big Red went from red to pink at the sight of Bonnie's necklace on this stranger. It was his version of pale. He placed his hand on his gun then removed it. As if he couldn't make up his mind, he pulled his gun. Instead of pointing it at them, he removed the bullets, placed them in his pocket then re-holstered his gun.

"Whatcha doing man?" Blondie asked. He and Goatee backed away from him.

"Trying not to kill the two of you."

Big Red looked at both of them. A fine sheen of sweat covered his upper lip and both his hands. He wiped them on his pants then he leaned against the door jam again.

"I don't understand." Goatee said truly confused by what was happening.

He and Blondie had been in close calls before. Generally there was a lot of talk, a search then they were released. Something was wrong here. Somehow they already knew about the murder. How, he couldn't figure out.

"I bet you don't. Let me put it this way. You should never commit a crime in a small town. If you do, you should know the town, it's people and your mark inside and out. See in small towns, everybody know everybody else. So well in fact, that we even know whose clothes you're wearing."

They looked at each other. "We ain't done nothing." Blondie yelled. "Nothing you hear!"

"I'm taking the two of you in."

"What's the charge man? We know our rights. You got to have a charge or we don't have to do nothing you say."

"You're not very smart are you boy?" Big Red asked. "If I want to take you in, all I have to do is haul your skinny little ass in."

"Are you going to tell us what your reasons are? Goatee asked.
"I did already."
"Yes but we're telling you we haven't stolen anything."
"That's right!" Blondie said.
"Since you're the brains of this little outfit, shut him up." Blondie looked at Goatee for a sign but got none. This actually confused Blondie causing him to shut up anyway.
"That's better. What you stole are the clothes on your backs. You might as well have worn something with his name on it. See, the shorts you're big mouth buddy are wearing has a stain on the left pocket.
"If you don't believe me, look for yourself. It looks like Mickey Mouse ears. Grace spotted those ears and called me. She would spot them since she feels she's the one responsible for them being there. Those shorts were stained last summer at the church day camp.
"Grace put a tube of acrylic paints on one of the benches. To keep from staining the bench, she placed the tube on a Mickey Mouse plate. Lawrence sat on that tube. It burst filling in the ears. To this day, when Lawrence wears those shorts we laugh. How's that for proof."
"That' don't prove nothing." Blondie said,
"By itself maybe not. But it's not by itself. The necklace you're wearing belongs to Lawrence's wife Bonnie. It's the only necklace like it in this town."
"Didn't have to get it from this town." Blondie said.
"True but if you didn't get it from Bonnie, you got it from somewhere else. It has a mother and her newborn child on it. Why would you be wearing it?" Big Red directed all his comments, questions and explanations to Goatee. He knew that Blondie would cause him to lose his temper and probably his control.
"Now the least you could have done to Bonnie is rob her. Somehow I know you didn't stop there. I hope she's alive. Or all the advice I gave you, you won't ever get to use."

Big Red looked at both of them for a moment. He waited for Goatee to signal Blondie. When he didn't, he spoke again this time to Grace.

"Did Bonnie come by here today?"

"Yes and she should be home by now. She has a big dinner planned..." Grace stopped, choking on her words.

"Grace I need you. Please try and keep it together. The phone is going to ring any minute now and I need you to answer it."

Goatee understood what Grace was feeling. He had a strong urge to fall apart too. He knew to do so would admit they were guilty. He wasn't quite ready to do that. There just might be hope for them yet.

Why had they stopped in this town anyway? So they had been caught. He wasn't really worried about that. What worried him was this big cop. He had ordered his men to turn their radios off. He'd never heard of that being done before. He was afraid of what it meant.

Goatee looked to see where Blondie was. He noticed that he had moved so that all but his head and shoulders were behind a shelf. Goatee couldn't see it but on that shelf there were cans of tuna, chicken, beans and vegetables.

Blondie was sure a good hard hit with one of those cans would slow Big Red down. Maybe even help them to get away. He reached for a can of tuna. He rolled that can over and over in his hand. He hefted it to get a good feel for it. All the while he was looking at Big Red. When he thought Big Red wasn't paying attention, he gripped the can prepared to throw it as hard as he could.

"You really want to piss me off don't you boy?" Big Red asked looking at Blondie.

"What? What's happening?" Grace asked.

Reality for her had finally set in and she was terrified. She hadn't noticed Blondie playing with the can goods. She'd been to busy trying to keep it together until the phone rang.

"I want to know what's going on Big Red."

"That big mouth kid thinks I'm stupid. He didn't think I was watching him. He's got a can of something in his hand. Must have been planning a hit and attack or a hit and run."

"My hands are empty." Blondie yelled holding his hand up. To keep from making any noise Blondie had put the can of tuna in his pocket.

"Look, how do you know we didn't get these clothes from the Salvation Army or a yard sale? You did say they were stained over a year ago. We do a lot of traveling. To off set cost, we buy our clothes that way. And how do you know I didn't find this necklace. The clasp is weak on it. I had to bite it to close it."

"You are good. Okay, that's a good point." Big Red said. "One problem with it, though, Bonnie hasn't had a yard sale and we don't have a Salvation Army here. Anyone in this town in need of help, we pull together and help them.

"As for the necklace, Bonnie had the clasp fixed on it already. I know because she showed it to me this morning. She was unhappy with the work because it didn't match the rest of the chain. That's how you knew it was broke. So try again."

That seemed to do it. Blondie and Goatee knew reasoning wasn't going to get them free. They also knew they needed to put some distance between them and this town. Blondie gave the signal. It told Goatee they had nothing to lose. Goatee obviously saw the rational in his actions because when Blondie charged Big Red, he charged right along beside him.

Grace saw the movement from her peripheral vision. She looked up and screamed. Her screams gave Blondie and Goatee hope. For when she screamed Big Red looked in her direction. The element of surprise, however, belonged to Big Red.

He had expected the two of them to do something foolish. He had hoped for it in fact. Much to their surprise, he was even prepared for it. It was one of the reasons he'd emptied his gun.

When Blondie and Goatee were within inches of Big Red, he stood semi crouched, like a football player. Both arms were crossed in front of his body. He didn't move at all. He let their momentum do the work and work it did.

The results were not pretty. Blondie and Goatee would have been luckier if they had run into the preverbal brick wall. The two of them hit Big Red hard. They bounced off of him harder.

"Grace stop your screaming!" Big Red yelled.

The tone of his voice worked better than the words themselves. She'd never heard Big Red yell. In fact, she'd never heard him raise his voice in the year and three months that she has been a member of The Walking Wounded Club. She stopped screaming.

"I told you I had everything under control. Relax. Okay? In fact, could you do me another favor?" She nodded meekly. "Call the station and see what's taking so long would ya?" Again Grace nodded. She picked the phone up with trembling hands.

"I knew you weren't the shining star of this outfit." Big Red said to Blondie. "But I expected you to have more sense. Now, I'm more convinced than ever that you're guilty. Your actions were that of desperate men."

"Big Red look!" Grace said pointing out the window. Her hand was trembling.

"Dial Grace. I'll handle this too." This time he smiled and that caused Grace to relax. She took a deep breath, steadied her hand and dialed.

Big Red looked at Blondie and Goatee. They both lay on the floor. Goatee was flat on his back looking up at the ceiling, his hands holding his head, his knees rocking from side to side. Blondie was on his hands and knees. One hand held his head. The other supported his weight. They weren't going anywhere.

Big Red opened the door wide enough to get George Kitchens attention. I wasn't sure why George Kitchens was in the town of The Walking Wounded. Grandma didn't think I should know. But George's reaction to Big Red's voice and his request let me know he belonged here fair and square.

"After noon George." Big Red said. "Do me a favor will ya? Come back and pay later. Better yet, I'll pay Grace. The next time you're in town, you can pay me. How's that?"

"Yes sir. Whatever you say. I can wait if you want me to Big Red. Do you just want me to come back?"

"That would help a lot George."

"Okay Big Red." George closed his tank, hung the pump back up and got in his car. He didn't look back. He headed straight for the street.

Before turning right, as he'd intended, a black and white pulled into the parking lot so fast that to keep from hitting George, the officer had to pull the wheels hard to the left. The right wheels momentarily left the ground.

This scared George so bad that he gunned his engine. This caused his car to stall. After numerous attempts to re-start the car, he flooded the engine. George Kitchens got out of his car and ran up the street. He crossed the street at one point to get to the next store. There, he ran inside. And it was there, that he stayed scared and shaken by the whole event.

The black and white looked as though it was going to run right into the store. Instead, it ran into the sidewalk. There, it came to such an abrupt stop that the car didn't seem to know it was supposed to be still. It shook violently as if it were seizing. Because of that shaking, Ron Jackson was trapped in the car. Every time he opened the door, it slammed shut.

"Grace please wait outside."

Ron Jackson was only twenty-seven. Already he was second in command. He was rather young to be second in command but it was a position he'd earned and was more than qualified for. Ron was fair, calm and he went by the book only if it was something that could come back to harm the town or the department.

In other words, he went by the book when dealing with outsiders. He used his heart when dealing with his friends and neighbors. Like Big Red, he was adored. Unlike Big Red, he was black.

This whole town had me confused but I didn't have time to think about that. Blondie and Goatee were sitting up and watching. I wasn't sure Big Red was watching them. I hoped he was.

For now, he stood holding the door open. He was standing sideways. This position made him vulnerable. He had back up now though. At least, I think he has back up. Ron Jackson sat in the now still car with his head on the steering wheel. He made no attempt to get out and for a moment, Big Red thought he would have to go get him.

When Grace opened the driver side door, Jackson looked up. Tears glistened his eyes and face. This sight caused Grace to cry too. To comfort her, Ron stepped out of the car and took Grace's hand. He patted it several times then he sat her down behind the wheel. He gently closed the door and walked quickly to where Big Red was standing.

"She's dead Big Red!" He whispered. "She's dead! She's dead!"

Blondie and Goatee looked at each other. After months of successfully doing what they considered to be their job, they'd been caught. They listened as Ron filled Big Red in on the details.

"The baby's dead too! Sweet Jesus Big Red, they're both dead! I've never seen anything like it. It's awful!"

With that comment, Ron Jackson seemed to see the scene in the Phillips house. He turned away from Big Red and gagged. Big Red patted Jackson's back and waited. When he was more composed, he continued.

"They're dead." Ron Jackson said again. "Blood. There's blood all over the kitchen." He tried not to cry. "Who could have…who would…I mean why?"

Big Red stood with one hand on Jackson's shoulder. He held the door open with his foot and he had his eyes on Blondie and Goatee. Now more than ever he wanted them to attack him. He wanted them to grab something, anything or try to escape. He wanted one of them to attempt to stand. He wanted any reason to hurt them. Neither moved.

I looked at Jackson and Big Red standing side by side. The town of The Walking Wounded was well protected. Jackson was six one and forty pounds lighter than Big Red. They would have made a football team all by themselves. Their size is where their similarities ended.

Ron wasn't officially a Walking Wounded member. That's because he was born in this town. Before today he has never seen a real crime. After today, he never wants to see another crime of this magnitude. He's a good cop and he loved his job. But before dealing with real crime on a day to day basis, he'd rather give up his badge.

"Who could have done this Red? Who?" Jackson asked.

"Get yourself together and come on in. I'll show you."

"Show me?" The comment had an affect closely akin to smelling salt. Jackson opened his eyes wide, spit to clear his mouth and his head, took a deep breath them stepped forward.

"Sonsofbitches in here."

Ron Jackson looked at Big Red then he looked inside the store. He had expected to see a monster. What he saw instead shocked him. Sitting on the floor were two young men, almost boys actually, looking back at him.

"Why Red?"

"I haven't gotten that far yet. Grace noticed Lawrence's shorts on that one and pushed the silent alarm. She didn't realize how bad things really were until she saw Bonnie's necklace on that one over there. He said pointing at Goatee.

"Why the veil?" Jackson asked still staring. For a moment, he felt disoriented. He even felt as if he were going to fall. He checked his knees to make sure they weren't locked then tried to make sense of it all.

"I don't want anybody else to pick this up. There are a lot of people out there that would like to make this their business. We don't want or need unwanted visitors at this time." Jackson looked at Big Red weighing his next question.

"I'm kinda confused Chief. Help me out here. What are you saying?"

"We're going to handle this ourselves. That's what I'm saying. Bonnie and her baby were our responsibility. I don't want the FBI in on this. I don't want a mob of reporters picking this town apart. But above everything else, I don't want these two to get away with murder.

"I don't want to see time and money wasted on sanity testing. I don't want to go to bed every night worrying about a mistrial. These two killed Bonnie and her baby. We know that. We don't need a whole mess of people losing site of that."

"Is there any chance we could be wrong about them? I mean, they look so normal. The ones responsible for the murders at the Phillips house weren't normal. They couldn't have been. Besides, what would their motive have been? Lawrence and Bonnie don't have any money.

"Was she raped?"

"Johnny said maybe. It's hard to tell with all the blood there.

"She was raped." Big Red said, sure of himself. "And I'll bet the motive wasn't money but hate." Jackson thought about that for a moment.

While Ron Jackson struggled to make sense of everything, another black and white pulled into the parking lot and parked behind the Cadillac. The driver of the black and white got out and walked to the caddy and peeked in. Without a warrant, he opened the backdoor. He reached in, retrieved the bag of bloody clothes and walked to the store.

"Ms. Grace." He said tipping his hat. He walked in leaving Grace to look at the trail of blood that leaked from the bag.

Ronnie Paine was the newly arrived officer. Ronnie carried himself as if he was a very cool character but closer inspection showed that behind that macho exterior was a caring person. His eyes were red, so was his nose. Like Ron Jackson, Ronnie Paine had been crying.

Ronnie was a jr. deputy. He had been off duty when Jennifer called him. After Ron Jackson, he was the second person on the scene. Now that the scene was crawling with fellow officers, he wanted to know how to be of further service. Not to mention, he wanted to get away from all that horror.

Looking at Ronnie, I was convinced that there was a protocol for all the officers of this town. One, you had to be big as hell. You had to be able to take on a tank. And you had to be part of the community. There were not outsiders on this force.

Paine walked in and looked around. He was armed; serious and ready to do business. Ronnie Paine's appearance here struck me as odd. Ronnie Paine was also black. I knew that the seventies were turbulent years for blacks and whites. Integration was signed into law but was not catching on without protest.

Yet, I was standing in a little store, in a little town, named God knows what and there were two black men already on the police department. Then there was Bonnie and Lawrence. Theirs was an interracial marriage that was accepted not just by Grace but according to Grandma by the whole town.

Where was I and how was this possible? I couldn't still be in America. Land of the free was only a slogan in the seventies. Maybe even now.

"Who owns that car out there?" Paine asked.

"Who knows? They were driving it though." Big Red said.

"Then I'd say they are the ones responsible for killing Bonnie and her baby." He placed the bag on the floor in front of Big Red.

Big Red and Jackson looked at the bag then looked away. Jackson looked at the two young men in front of him. Again, he asked himself how they could look so normal. How they could have done what they did to Bonnie and be human? It wasn't possible. He was sure if they pulled their skin away there would be a monster underneath.

Paine looked at the two murders and saw monsters anyway. He wasn't fooled by the human look they had assumed. They were monsters and nothing could convince him otherwise. He'd already seen what they were capable of.

Big Red simply wondered how it could have happened in this town. Nothing of this magnitude has happened in this town since it's conception. He shook his head and looked at Blondie and Goatee. He felt a hate for those two he didn't know he was capable of.

Paine looked at the bag he'd placed in front of Big Red. It was leaking. A small puddle of blood formed beneath it. He went to a shelf, one that was still standing and took a box of trash bags off. With the help of Big Red, he double bagged the bloody clothes to make sure there was no more seepage. When they were done, Big Red turned to Ron Jackson.

"Still think we have the wrong suspects." He asked. Before Jackson could answer, Paine spoke again.

"There's more. We found it after you left Ron. The words, 'I just rid the world of two more niggers' was written on two of the mirrors." Paine was silent for a moment while he let that information set in. He looked at the mess on the floor then asked. "Is all this damage you're doing Big Red?"

"No, not all mine. They helped."

"I see. When things settle down, I'll come back and help Ms. Grace clean up." He said then looked at Ron and Big Red again. "Does any of that sound familiar to either of you?"

"No. should it?" Big Red said.

"Yes it should." Ron said remembering. "We recently got a memo from the FBI in reference to some killings in South Carolina and Virginia. I put a copy of it on your desk. The memo warned us to be on the look out."

"I'm not surprised. Maybe now you'll understand the veil better." Big Red said looking at first Ronnie then Ron.

"My God Red, I've never seen anything this ugly before." Ron said. It's hard to believe these two are responsible for all this ugliness."

"It will get uglier if this gets out." Ronnie said. Big Red nodded.

"How did this happen? Who opened the door and let the outside in? Ron asked.

"Not the outside." Big Red corrected. "Just those two. It's up to us to make sure that the door closes and stays that way. Or the outside really will get in." He looked at his watch. "Let's get these two settled in. We still have a lot of unpleasant work to do.

"I've never liked this part of the job. It's the part that doesn't get any better or easier with time. How do you tell a man his wife and child are gone? One fell swoop and his whole family is gone. Then there is Tina and Jake." He said shaking his head. He turned to Blondie and Goatee.

"Let's go." Neither of them moved.

"Because of the two of you, we aren't having a very good day. All we need is a reason; any reason and we'll be forced to use force." Ronnie Paine said. That got them moving.

When Goatee got to Big Red, he put his hand out to stop him. "Turn around." Goatee did what he was ordered to do and Bonnie's necklace was removed. When Blondie got to Big Red, he simply held his hand out. Blondie reached into his pocket and removed the can of tuna. He gave it to Big Red.

Big Red flanked Goatee. Ron flanked Blondie. Ronnie took up the rear. It was at that point that he saw the back of the shorts Blondie was wearing.

"Jesus Christ! You might as well have worn something with Lawrence written across the front. Everyone in this town knows about Mickey."

"So they have been told." Big Red said.

"Lawrence told me that paint went straight through to his skin. He walked around with an imprint of Mickey Mouse ears on his butt for three days. He told me the paint wouldn't come off no matter what he tried." Big Red and Ron smiled as they remembered.

While the three of them were reminiscing, Blondie and Goatee looked at each other. Neither gave a signal. Neither could read the other's facial expression. It was the first time in ten years that this has happened. They formulated those signals and improved them to perfection over the years. Now they couldn't read the simplest of expression. Of course having three big cops surround them didn't help.

"Matty?"
"Yes Grandma."
"How are you?"
"A better question would be, how are you?"

"Better." Actually, she did sound better. She was still wheezing but not panting.

"Grandma what are the chances of that ever happening again? I mean how many people would have been that observant. If Grace hadn't been responsible for that stain, would she have even noticed?"

"Oh yea of little faith. I believe Grace would have noticed."

"If Bonnie had been my best friend, I believe her murders would have gotten away. I'm not a very observant person."

"Can you be so sure? You've never had a best friend. If you'd had one, you would know no boundaries when it comes to protecting them. It's kinda like what you feel for Chris."

"Really? I have a lot to learn."

"And learn you shall."

"So Big Red, what's your plan?" I heard Paine ask. Regretfully, Grandma was gone.

"The plan for now is to take care of our dead. After that, I think it best to let Lawrence decide what the plan will be."

Ron and Ronnie looked at Big Red then each other and nodded. They liked the plan. Goatee and Blondie looked at Big Red then each other. They had never heard of such a plan but they were sure they didn't like it.

BLINK! I found myself inside the police station. Ron was escorting Blondie into his cell while Ronnie was escorting Goatee into his cell.

At the time, they were the only prisoners. In fact, most of the time the cells stand empty, their doors open and unlocked. However, Ron and Ronnie's key slid into the well-oiled lock and turned as easily as if they were used every day. When in truth, the last time either cell had been occupied was four months ago.

Once Blondie and Goatee were locked away, they stood at the bars and watched in disbelief as everyone started for the door.

"Hey wait a minute! You can't do this!" Blondie yelled. "We know our rights. You're supposed to read us our rights. You never did."

Big Red looked at Ron and Ronnie. All three of them shrugged but didn't answer. They turned back towards the door.

"I want to make a phone call! You hear me! I get one phone call and I want it now!"

Neither of them turned. Neither of them spoke. They just kept walking. Soon Blondie, Goatee and myself were looking at a closed door.

BLINK! I found myself back outside the Phillips house. The black and white carrying Big Red and the two Rons hadn't arrived yet. Johnny Stevens, a paramedic of eighteen years, stood by his ambulance waiting. He knew he couldn't move the bodies until Big Red gave him clearance nor did he want too.

Carl Douglas, another one of the town's deputies was also on hand. He was busy placing yellow police tape around the Phillips house. His other co-workers were keeping a small crowd of spectators' back. Nothing unusual here.

Why had I been sent ahead I wondered? I got no answer. Grandma was with me less and less now. I hated that. My first real friend and I would lose her before I got the chance to know her.

About five minutes after I arrived, I saw Big Red's black and white approaching. Paul Solomon, yet another police officer and Johnny went to meet the car. Paul nodded at his boss and co-workers but didn't speak. This struck Big Red as profound because by nature Paul was a chatterbox. Shutting him up was generally the problem.

Paul was the youngest man on the force but right now he looked anything but. Like everyone else, he had been deeply affected by the murders and the loss of a close friend. Johnny was fifty-years-old and a transplant like Big Red. He too looked older. His shirt was wet with sweat, as was his brow.

"Big Red no one around here has seen the likes of this. I have to admit I haven't either and I thought I'd seen it all."

Johnny got straight to the point. There was no room for greetings. Besides, I couldn't think of a greeting that would fit.

Big Red nodded. "The guys told me I'd never believe it."

"I'm still trying to believe it. She was desperate Big Red. I'm sure of that. Not for herself either but for her baby." Johnny said.

"It looks like she tried to put the baby back inside." Paul said finally breaking his silence. "Why did they have to torture her? Why did they have to bother her at all? I don't understand Big Red. Why?" He asked truly trying to understand something that could not be explained.

Big Red got out of the car shaking his head. He placed his hand on Paul's shoulder but said nothing. Paul needed and appreciated that big hand. The gesture said, 'I don't understand either. I wish I did. I wish I could change it all.'

Paul understood what he meant and placed his hand on Big Red's and nodded. Ron and Ronnie watched them from inside the car. There was no reason to get out. There was nothing for them to do anyway.

Big Red looked at the sky. He wanted to appreciate the beauty of it but he couldn't. Not with what he knew he was about to face. He took his hat off, wiped at the sweat that had formed on his forehead then replaced it.

It was hot. The middle of July. In fact, he realized while standing there that it was the hottest July he could remember. But the heat wasn't what had caused the sweat and he knew it.

He looked at the house. It was the same house that he had visited just two days earlier. He'd come by to return an empty tin to Bonnie only to have it refilled with his favorite, chocolate chip cookies. It now sat on his kitchen counter. Empty again.

His plan had been to wait a while before coming back. He didn't want to appear greedy but if the truth were told, that tin of cookies was empty the same day. Now, she would never fill it again.

She will never come by the station just to say hello. She will never kiss his cheek after he place his hat on her head. There were a lot of nevers. More than he wanted to think about.

He looked up again. He wanted something to focus on other than the truth. He focused on Carl Douglas. Carl was not only a deputy but Lawrence's cousin. What he must me going through.

"Carl we have the two responsible for Bonnie's murder." He spoke in a gentle fatherly voice.

"I know that Big Red."

"So why are you sealing off the house?"

"Needed something to do. The longer I sat still, the more I thought about what she must have went through. I can only guess but that was enough to get me on my feet. I wanted to help catch them. Since they'd already been caught, I had to do something.

"The next time I think of Bonnie, I don't want to think of the pain and fear she must have felt her last hours. I don't want to remember her like she is now." Carl stopped and looked at the house.

He took a deep breath then said a prayer for Bonnie, her baby and his cousin Lawrence for all to hear. No one said anything until he was done. Then there were Amen's all around.

"Big Red I know you're no stranger to violence but we are. There is no violence here. Never has been…not until today that is. Everyone here gets along with everyone else.

"I was born and raised here. I can't even remember fighting on the playground. We've always thought there was enough fighting on the outside. No one wanted it here.

"Good Lord Big Red, they used that word. You know the one I mean. I was taught as a child not to use that word. God would be very very angry if I did. It's a bad word. I've never even heard it used here. But it's written twice in that house." Carl was quiet for a moment while he sought and found his wrinkled handkerchief.

Big Red started to say something then stopped. He decided to let Carl get off his chest what he needed to. He knew he was speaking what everyone else was feeling. Including himself. Carl's speech was therapeutic. He knew therapy had to start somewhere. Right here, right now was as good a place to start as any.

"Big Red everyone knows everyone else here. I'm not just saying that. We really do. Before coming here, did you know all of your neighbors?" Carl asked but he didn't stop long enough for an answer.

"Of course you didn't. You didn't know them and what's worse you disliked most of them. Not here Big Red. I mean I'd truly be hard pressed to find something bad to say about someone in this town." He looked at the ground then back at Big Red.

"Do you know how many times I've had dinner here Big Red? Not just here but at all my neighbors house's. Color has never been an issue here.

"Jesus Big Red, my mama just finished knitting a blanket for that baby. What am I going to tell her? What is she supposed to do with it now, bury him in it? Jesus Big Red, wait till you see her. See what she went through. What they did to her.

"Why did she have to suffer like that?" He yelled then kicked the tire on the patrol car. "Why did they do it? Why?" He yelled at no one in particular then he slammed his fist down on the roof of the black and white. He put his head down and cried.

"Carl go on home." Big Red said placing a big supportive arm around Carl's shoulder. "Tell Ms Lilly what's happened."

"I need to be here. This is my job." He said tears staining his face.

"When you're sure your mother's okay, you can come on back. Go on. Go home." Carl handed Big Red the yellow tape and started up the street.

His mother lived three streets over, as did he. Earlier in the year he bought the house next to hers. He was to get married soon. With his house next door, he would be able to take care of his house and be close enough to take care of her when she needed him. We watched him until he disappeared between some houses then we turned our attention back to the Phillips house.

"Big Red I know you have to go in there. I don't want to go back in there but I will if you want me to come with you." Johnny said.

"Thanks Johnny. Bonnie was my Godchild. I'd rather be alone." Johnny nodded.

He, like everyone else standing around, knew that Bonnie was one of many of Big Red's Godchildren. Big Red loved children, had wanted a few of his own. In fact, he fathered one but didn't know if it was a boy or a girl. Nor did he know where that child was.

Back in the late sixties Big Red had been married for two years. He'd thought of himself as a loving husband. He was definitely a faithful one.

The problems in his marriage started midway the second year. First his co-workers taunted him then he was taunted by his wife. All the taunting came because Big Red worked hard to solve his cases. He had the best record in the department.

This made his fellow officers mad with envy. Big Red was so good because he didn't care what the crime or what color the victim. They all got his undivided attention.

This undivided attention kept him away from home often. When his wife tried to reach him at work, she was never patched through. She was often told he never showed up for work. It took its toll on the young marriage. One day he came home, she along with everything he owned was gone.

With nothing holding him in New York, he got in his car and left. He had no destination. He'd just had enough, so where he ended up didn't matter. Where he ended up was in the town of The Walking Wounded fifteen years ago. He stayed.

Big Red was liked by all. He was loved by most, especially the children. There wasn't one he didn't try to help with something, from riding a bike to shooting hoops. None of them forgot his birthday or him at Christmas.

Most years he had to take out a loan to buy all his kids Christmas and birthday presents. Loans he spent most weekends working off. But he didn't mind.

Big Red started for the house. His wide shoulders were slumped his head was down. He couldn't remember the last time he'd felt this low. He stepped to the door and stopped. Before even opening it, he could smell the blood.

Once inside the front door, I watched as he crossed himself. I walked beside him dreading looking at the death scene again. At least, I wasn't alone. I was glad for that. At the kitchen door, he crossed himself again then went in. The door was as far as I could go. I was not allowed to enter only Big Red was.

One step inside the kitchen door, he looked to his left and drew in a deep breath. He put his big hand in his mouth and bit down on it. Hard. He took a step toward Bonnie as a deep racking sob came from somewhere deep inside his chest.

He stepped over the trail of blood that she'd made during her journey to get to her baby and knelt beside her.

"Dear Lord please forgive me. I'm so sorry." He said. "I promised to take care of this town. I begged you for some place nice to go. In exchange, I promised to care for and protect everyone of its people. I have failed you Lord! I have failed my baby girl!" He cried in anguish.

I tried to look in. I was allowed. I watched as he bowed at Bonnie's feet as if she had been royalty. I watched as he sobbed until his whole body shook. I watched him and thought about my future.

One day I'll fall in love. One day I'll lose that love. On that day I'll look back to this day and I'll know what Big Red and this town was feeling.

I know I loved my father and I hurt when he died but I had been eight. I reacted like an eight-year-old would react. I was angry with my dad for dying. Angry because we wouldn't be able to do all the things we had planned. Angry because with him gone Wayne was able to step in and take over. I was just plain angry.

I've not loved anyone since my father nor have I allowed anyone to get close enough to love me. If I were to die right now, there would only be one person who cared. Only one person who would miss me. There would be only one person who would have anything good to say about me. There was only one person who tried to protect me. That one person would be Chris.

Big Red said another prayer, crossed himself again then stood. "They'll pay for this Bonnie. I promise you they'll pay." He stepped back over the trail of blood then walked out of the kitchen. He stopped in the living room, looked around then he walked out to the porch.

Once outside, his knees gave way and he started to fall. To everyone, it looked like he was swaying. I stepped forward to help him. Using all my strength, I pushed against him. I held him up until he was able to ease himself to the steps where he flopped down unceremoniously. He never looked at me and I wasn't sure if he'd been able to feel me pushing against him.

Paul, Ron and Ronnie joined him on the steps. Johnny stayed by the car. He knew he would have to go in soon enough and he wasn't going near the house until he had to.

"Carl is Lawrence's cousin." Ron Jackson said.

"I know."

"He's really taking this hard. He and Lawrence are close, like brothers. Both of them are only children. He knows how much this is going to destroy Lawrence." Ron Jackson finished.

"Bonnie is the only girl Lawrence has ever loved. Everyone in town knows that. God, I can still remember what he was like back when we were kids. Lawrence used to wait for Bonnie to finish her piano practice. He used to follow her around like he was a lost puppy. He had it bad." Ronnie Paine said then gave a laugh. "Remember" He said then stopped.

Ronnie had been so angry up to this point that he hadn't let himself really cry. He had been bent and determined to keep it together until they caught the culprits. That part of their job was done. Remembering caused him to let his defenses down and he dropped his head. The sobs that came from his chest ignited Big Red's, Jackson's and Paul's. Soon there were four grown men crying. Five, if you count me.

Johnny turned his back to the officers. My guess is he cried too. The crowd didn't know exactly what to make of this but they knew it wasn't good. This made most of them cling to each other for support.

"Where's Sidney today? Does any one know?" Big Red asked when he was able to speak without crying.

"He went out to old man Mayfield's place. Johnny ran into him this morning. Old man Mayfield's heifer was getting ready to deliver." Ron said.

"Does he know?"

"Yeah. Carl got in touch with him. He told Carl he would go get Sarah. Together they would go by and tell Tina. After that, they would bring her over here.

"We tried the construction site where Jake and Lawrence are working today. But the Forman said that he wouldn't try to reach them unless he was told what the problem was. I told him it was an emergency and that it was police business. He still refused. So I told him to go fuck himself." Paul said.

Generally Big Red would have reprimanded Paul then laughed but not today. He just sat staring at his hands.

"I guess I should go over to Tina's and help Sidney and Sarah." Big Red said but he didn't move.

"Bonnie was also an only child. She was the only child Tina and Jake could have actually. They were looking forward to this grandchild and maybe two or three others."

No one spoke. No one had to. The silence said more than either of them could have. Three families and a whole town's feeling of well being were destroyed today because of one hateful act.

"What tipped Grace off?" Paul asked.

"They were wearing Lawrence's clothes. On closer inspection, she noticed that one of them was wearing Bonnie's necklace."

"Good ole Grace." Ron Jackson said with real admiration for her. They all nodded in agreement. They all knew that without her, they might have never found out who was responsible for this horrendous act.

"Her grandma had that necklace made for her." Ronnie Paine said more to himself than to anyone in particular.

"Everyone whose anyone knows that Bonnie got that necklace for her twelfth birthday. She really cherished that necklace. Shortly after receiving it, her grandma died. She was so proud of it. She showed me the inscription once. But I can't remember what it said."

"You are so special that you can only be a blessing from God." Big Red said. Everyone looked at him. He didn't look up. He had remembered it because he had believed it to be so.

I thought about my own life again. I was a doctor. I've come in contact with many people, both as a student and as an intern but there was no doubt that this woman had touched lives in a way I never did. In a way I never wanted too.

For that she was loved. For that she will be missed. Her death had heads bowed, eyes wet. Her death was doing something else. It was bringing a town that was already close closer. It reminded them of their love and why they had been brought here in the first place.

"Grandma?" I asked speaking her name so softly I didn't think I'd spoken it at all.

"Yes child." She panted. She was struggling to breathe again. I hesitated to ask my question.

"Where is this place?"

"It's your new home."

She coughed. I heard rattling in her throat as she gasped for air. I held my breath afraid she wouldn't ever take another breath.

"What makes you think they'll want me?" I had to ask. I didn't want to bother her but I had to ask. "I have done nothing to be proud of. I don't have anything to offer them."

"They're not there to judge you child." She spoke fast, trying to say everything before running out of air. "They aren't there to question you either." She coughed another watery cough. "If you show up, they'll just accept you."

"You really helped to kill those two?"

"Yes."

"Is that why you asked me if two wrongs make a right?"

"Does it?"

"Can I answer that question after I have seen everything?"

"I think that's a very wise decision Matty."

"Wise? Me wise?" I asked unable to help feeling just a little bit of pride sweep over me. "I bet you didn't think I was very wise at five fifteen." I said laughing.

"That's cause you weren't." She too laughed then coughed. Something about us laughing felt right.

"She died an awful death."

"Yes Matty she did."

"How are you holding up? You sound awful. I really should come on back and help you." Her heart rate was thirty-eight.

I didn't know what time it was. For all I knew, it could have been three p.m. But my watch still read five fifteen. So it was five fifteen.

"I'm fine Matty. Thank you for asking." She said, this time without coughing, panting or gasping for air. Then she laughed again.

So did I. I didn't have to ask her how she was feeling. I wanted to ask her. I wanted to know. It felt good to be doing things because they were the right things to do. I felt good.

"I've felt things I can't remember ever feeling before." I said serious again. "Most of them I didn't like."

"Some you did."

"Not enough. But at least I can feel. That counts right?" But she was gone again. Her heart rate was now thirty-seven.

Nothing changed while I was speaking with Grandma. It's like time stopped for a minute but only for a minute. I heard a rumble then followed Paul's finger as he pointed down the road.

A red Ford pick up pulled to the curb behind Big Red's black and white. There were three passengers in the truck. The first one out came from the passenger side. It was Sarah Phillips. She was a petite lady weighing no more than one hundred pounds. She had dark brown hair and eyes. The rims of those eyes were red.

Getting out of the driver side and coming around the front of the truck was Sidney Phillips. Sidney was just the opposite of his wife. Where she was dark, he was blond with blue eyes. His face was lined by years out in the sun. His hands big and hard yet when he reached for Tina, I could tell they were gentle.

Unlike Sidney and Sarah Phillips, Tina's eyes were dry. She refused to cry. She refused to believe that her baby was dead.

I looked at Tina Williams for a long time. While it's true she was an attractive woman, I found it hard to believe she was Bonnie's mother. For one thing, she didn't look old enough to have a child as old as Bonnie had been. For another, they looked nothing alike. The only thing they seemed to have in common was that they were both black.

Bonnie was tall and slim. She was the kind of woman other ladies wanted to look like. Even pregnant she'd turned heads. Her mother was short, about five feet even and she carried about thirty pounds more than she could handle. She had a very dark complexion and she wore her hair cropped short.

Tina Williams got out of the truck and looked at the tape surrounding her daughter's house. Then she looked at Big Red. I didn't know Tina's story and Grandma didn't think I needed to know or didn't have the strength to tell me.

I did know that she and her husband were part of the Walking Wounded. It showed in her eyes. It showed in the hurt that she was trying to keep at bay by not believing. It showed in how she held her shoulders square and her head up high. But it showed.

Tina looked at Big Red, who had some how found the strength to stand. This man who had once reminded me of a charging bull, now looked like the middle aged man that he was and the old man that he was to become. In one day, life had caught up with him.

"Tina…" He started then stopped. He'd broken the news to many families but never to a family as close to him as this one. He didn't know what to say.

"No." She whispered. She dropped her head for the briefest of moments then looked up again. She took a deep breath then said. "I want to see her." Her voice strong, her head high again.

"Tina why don't you wait for Jake?"

"I want to see her now." It was a request not a demand. "Take me to her Big Red. Please take me to my daughter." She said continuing to stare straight ahead. She was focused and unwavering.

"It's an awful scene Tina."

"I will never hear my daughters voice or see her smile again. I will never feel her arms around me. I will never hear her tell me how much she loves me. That, Big Red is an awful scene." Without saying another word, Big Red took Tina by the arm and led her up the porch stairs and into the living room.

There he stopped. He was stalling but he didn't want her to know it. He thought it would be best if Jake went in with her. But he could only stall for so long. He wasn't sure if Jake and Lawrence even knew. If they didn't, it could be another couple of hours before they got home.

Tina stared into the kitchen. With or without him, she was going in. She made this clear by walking away from him. He caught up and walked beside her.

Right behind them was Sarah and Sidney. At the door, Sidney turned to Sarah. "Are you sure you want to do this?"

"No. But I have to." She said.

Tina Williams took a deep breath and stepped forward. She looked straight ahead then as if having to will herself to do so, she looked to the left. Her only reaction was to cover her mouth with her hand. She stood like that for about a minute then she slowly removed her hand. In one step, she was at Bonnie's side.

Once there, whatever forces responsible for holding Tina Williams together abandon her so totally, she literally dropped to her knees. She leaned over Bonnie and her grandson and let out a painful, soul retching sob.

Big Red stood in the kitchen doorway with his head down. Sidney went to the door tentatively and looked in. One look was more than enough for him. He turned to his wife and pushed her against the wall outside of the kitchen.

"Please stay here. I'm going to get Tina."

"No Sidney! You stay here. I'll get Tina. If Lawrence shows up, he'll need you out here." Big Red said. "Sidney….." He said then stopped, trying to choose his words carefully. "Don't let him in there."

"I'm not sure if I can stop him."

"Go get her. Go get her out of there." Sarah said able to here Tina but not able to see her.

Sarah was able to speak only between her sobs. She had become so frantic she was pacing back and forth. She was running her hands through her hair and crying so hard her body shook. Big Red watched her. Sidney tried to stop her long enough to put his arms around her. She wouldn't let him.

"Go get her Red!" She yelled.

Big Red turned to go into the kitchen. SLAM! Lawrence burst into the living room, jumped over the fallen couch then he ran straight for the kitchen, where Big Red and Sidney tried to stop him.

"Son you don't want to go in there."

"Let go of me!" He yelled, pushing both his father and Big Red back like he was two and they were one. "Bonnie!" He yelled.

"Let me go!" He hissed through clenched teeth. When he spoke those words, spittle came out and landed on his chin. "Bonnie!" He yelled continuing to push the barricade backwards. "God damn it Dad let me go!"

SLAP! Sidney stepped back as if he had been slapped physically rather than literally. In all of Lawrence's twenty-five years, his father had never heard him cuss. Let alone cuss at him. Sidney's shock gave Lawrence the edge he needed. With his dad out of the way, Big Red was easier to handle.

"She wouldn't want you to see her like that." A voice said. It belonged to Tina.

Lawrence stopped struggling. All eyes turned in the direction that the voice had originated. There in the doorway, seeming to stand taller than her five feet was Tina Williams.

Tina stood with tearstains on her face bloodstains on her hands, her knees and blouse. Jake stepped around Lawrence so that he could see his wife. Slowly he approached the kitchen. He started past her.

"No Jake!" She said looking him in the eyes.

Her voice strong once more, belying the fact that she had just wept with sheer abandonment. She then looked at Lawrence.

"Bonnie loved you two more than life itself. Even me and I know that child loved me. I also know that she wouldn't want either of you to see her like this. What's left in that kitchen is not our baby. What's in that kitchen is not the woman you love."

She looked down at her hands then the rest of her and trembled as the tears fought to get out. Jake grabbed her and pulled her to him. Together they cried. Red assumed watch at the kitchen door. At first, Lawrence made no move towards the kitchen. He stood watching the strongest person he had ever met cry. Lawrence frowned then slowly started for the kitchen.

"Son please don't."

"I have to. I have to see what they did to her." Sidney placed his hand on his son's shoulder.

Lawrence looked at the hand then at his father. Sidney had never seen his son like this. But he knew that if the shoe were on the other foot, he would be angry enough to go through an army. So he removed his hand.

"I'll go with you." He said.

"Please understand dad when I tell you I have to do this by myself." Sidney nodded then stepped aside. Big Red did the same, as Lawrence approached the door.

Lawrence stopped long enough to look at Tina. She stood in Jake's arms and shook her head. He looked at his mother, who was still standing outside the kitchen. She had stopped pacing and was holding her hands to her chest.

Her eyes pleaded with him not to go in. Disregarding both sets of parents, he stepped into the kitchen doorway. He took one look at the blood on the floor, the trail that led to his wife and son, and finally he looked at his wife and son. Then he turned and walked out.

He walked past Ronnie, Ron and Carl, now back, who was standing outside of the front door. He walked past Paul and Johnny who were standing at the bottom of the steps, straight to the truck that he and Jake had arrive in. He got in it facing forward, eyes straight. Everyone followed.

"Son why don't you come back to the house with your mother and me?" Sidney asked.

"If it's alright with Mom and Dad Williams, I'd like to stay in Bonnie's old room."

"Son her room is…"

"Just the way she left it. I know. She told me you could never bring yourself to get rid of her things. She loved that room. I love her. Right now, that's all I got." Both Jake and Tina nodded. Lawrence stepped out of the truck to let Tina in then he returned to his place.

"You two gonna follow us?" Jake asked.

"Yeah. We're right behind you." Sidney said then turned to Big Red. "Where will you be? We need to talk."

"I'm gonna check on the prisoners then I'll join you at Jake and Tina's."

BLINK! Just like that I was back at the jail. Blondie rose from his cot and walked to the bars. He watched as Big Red and his crew walked in. They all dragged their feet as if they carried a heavy load. No one spoke. No one was in the mood to be spoken to either.

"Well it's about time you showed up. I want you to know that everyone of my rights have been violated and I plan to sue this, this pigsty for everything you got." Blondie said.

When no one responded, he took this to mean he had the upper hand and he continued. "I've been keeping track." He said. "You left us alone for two hours and twelve minutes. You never offered to let us use the phone. And you never read us our rights."

"That's what you gonna tell your lawyer?" Carl asked.

Big Red looked at Carl then shook his head. He wondered how Carl could allow this jackass to draw him into a conversation.

"Damn straight that's what I'm going to tell him. Now give me a phone. I want to make a call." He demanded.

"We really should do things by the book Big Red." Carl said standing and reaching for the phone.

Everyone in the room frowned at him, even me. What was he doing? Big Red was about to ask him just that when Carl bent down and disconnected the phone from the wall. He walked over and handed Blondie the phone.

Blondie was so surprised by what had happened that he took the phone. Carl walked back to his desk and sat down. Blondie wasn't the only one shocked, we all were. Ron Jackson was the first to laugh.

"All right Carl!" Jackson said. Paul and Ronnie laughed too.

When it finally hit Blondie what had just happened, he slammed the phone to the floor breaking it. At that, Big Red started laughing. Carl, who reacted out of frustration and pain at having just witnessed his family struggling with each other, had not given the phone to Blondie as a joke. However, seeing it for what it was, he couldn't help but laugh too.

"Carl's right." Ron said. "Here's a book Big Red. We are planning to throw the book at them aren't you?"

"You bet we are."

"That's not funny you back woods pile of shit!" Blondie yelled. "You just wait. I want to see whose laughing when my lawyer gets here."

"Who's your lawyer boy?" Big Red asked.

"You'll know as soon as he gets here."

"He know where you are boy?" Goatee's eyes widen immediately. He understood where Big Red was headed.

"How in the hell is he supposed to know? You simple moron." Big Red looked at Blondie then at his deputies. He smiled then turned his attentions to Goatee.

"Your friend's not too bright is he?" Goatee didn't respond. He just looked at the broken phone.

"Let me explain something to you boy. You wanta know why you haven't used the phone? You wanta know why you haven't been allowed to call your lawyer?" Blondie didn't answer although Big Red paused for one.

"And he had the nerve to call me a simple moron. Let me break it down for you boy. Nobody knows where you are because we don't want anybody to know where you are." Blondie opened his mouth to speak but stopped to think. When reality hit him, his eyes opened wide and his face drained of all color.

"I'd say the light just came on." Ron Jackson said.

"Good" said Paine. "Then you'll understand that you have no rights in this town."

"You get only what we give you." Carl added.

"Say your prayers boys. You came into this town, a nice little quiet town, by the way, and you caused a lot of pain." Ron said.

"Fuck ya'll!" Blondie yelled. "We didn't do nothing. All we did was get rid of a couple of niggers. Why you making such a fuss over that? If you weren't wearing that uniform and if the government would stay out of decent white folk's homes and offices, you would be thanking us.

"Hey!" Blondie said after thinking for a moment. "With the help of the three of you, we could give those two a good working over. We could make them quit the force and dare either of them to tell why.

"We could make them say they were responsible for our escape and you could let the families deal with them. You name it. Or if you just want a good show, we'll work em over while you watch. All you have to do is let us go."

"You'd do that for us?" Big Red asked smiling.

"Sure we would." Blondie said also smiling.

"Ron, Ronnie what do you think of that?"

"I think the son of a bitch is crazy." Ronnie said. Ron Jackson didn't answer at all. He just stared at Blondie like he was looking a something with two heads.

"You think?" Carl asked.

"I know the son of a bitch is crazy." Ronnie corrected.

"That's better." Carl said.

"I think I'll have to say no to your offer boy. Thank you just the same though. Don't think we don't appreciate you for asking." Big Red said.

"Cause we really don't appreciate it. What we really don't appreciate is you coming here and trying to spread you hate. We don't appreciate you killing one of our friends. Most of all, we don't appreciate the two of you."

"What the fuck is going on here? I know. I musta fell down and knocked myself out. I must have been in a fucking coma and now I'm in the fucking twilight zone." Blondie said.

"I can explain all of this to you." Big Red said then stopped. "Maybe I can't. This is kinda like the twilight zone isn't it?"

"Funny! You stupid son of a bitch."

"You know boy; I just might have to wash your mouth out before this is over. And believe me." Big Red said stepping to the cell and opening the door. "I'm just the one to do it." Blondie backed up and out of Big Red's reach.

"You're full of piss and vinegar aren't you boy? Except when it comes to helpless pregnant women." When Blondie didn't respond, Big Red closed the door and locked it.

"What Big Red is trying to say?" Carl said. "Is that the government is not making us do anything we don't want to do. Ronnie and Ron earned the right to be on this team. They're good cops and even better friends."

"As far as the government is concerned, this is an all white department. They get what they want. We get what we need. We like it best when we are left alone." Ron Jackson said. "There have been black police on this force as far back as the twenties."

"That's not possible!" Blondie said. "How is that possible?"

"We make the rules here." Big Red said. "We have our own city counsel, mayor and board of education. The founder of this town came over from Europe back in the nineteen hundreds.

"He was appalled by the brutality of slavery and thought all men should be free. He bought this land and invited people to come and stay here. The only requirement was to feel as he did.

"That's how it got started. No one knows exactly how it evolved to where we are now. Some of us, like the young men you see here today, were born here. Others, like myself, fell through a hole of some sort and ended up here."

Blondie and Goatee stood staring at Big Red. "Are you making this up? Goatee asked.

"No I'm not. For ninety-nine years, this town has watched the world go by but has never wanted to join it. For ninety-nine years, we have never had a crime anywhere close to the one that the two of you committed.

"We have never needed to call in the FBI. We have never invited reporters to write up our festivals. We don't advertise nor do we do anything to draw attention to ourselves. And for ninety-nine years, this town has known nothing but peace and love."

"Hey man, you hear that? We made history." Blondie said to Goatee.

"Yes. And for that you will pay." Carl said. At that, he stood. "They're waiting for us over at the Williams place aren't they?" He said then walked. We followed.

BLINK! I found myself outside again. This time I was outside of the Williams residents. I was sitting between Jake and Sidney, one step down from Lawrence. This practically put me in his lap.

According to Jake's watch, it was now six thirty. My watch remained stuck at five fifteen. I wasn't the only one at the Williams house. There were many neighbors sitting on the Williams front lawn. I was surprised to see all the people present, with more showing up. Most with food.

"What you gonna do with them Big Red?" Jake asked.

"For now nothing." All eyes were focused on him. All ears toned in to his voice. His voice echoed over the silence as if he were using a microphone. "We have to take care of our children first." That comment met with many nods and a lot of approval.

"Then, I thought I'd let Lawrence decide what to do with them."

Again, this met with nods of approval and agreement. Lawrence didn't look up or respond. Something on his shoe seemed to be more important.

I looked to see what it was. There, on the outer rim of his left work boot was blood. He shifted his attention to his right work boot. It was clean. He looked back at his left work boot.

Jesus! I thought. What was he thinking? I waited for a revelation but did not get one.

I couldn't even begin to guess what must be going through his mind. I never wanted to be in the position to find out. I know we all bitch about the bad things in our lives. I know I do. But what could be worse than looking at blood on your shoe, knowing it came from your now deceased wife?

"I had all my officers turn off their radios today." Big Red went on saying. "This was to guarantee that we didn't attract any outsiders." More nods, signifying more approval. "So it goes without saying that no one is to discuss this outside of here." He stopped to look at the growing crowd.

"Is there anyone here that can't agree with this decision? We don't want to step on any toes. But we all know if reporters start filing in here, life, as we know it will be over. They'll pick us apart. They'll ask questions we don't want to answer and questions we can't answer." Frank Stanton said.

Frank was the mayor and has been for ten years. He fell into the position after his father, Frank Stanton SR, died. The town figured he had worked with his father long enough to know all the ins and outs and there was no need to train anyone else.

Frank has three daughters. The middle one works with him. Everyone knows that if anything ever happened to Frank, she would be the next to take over.

"Not only that." Old man Mayfield pitched in. "With the way the world is now, those two will only get a slap on the hand. They'll be told not to do it again. They'll be turned lose on the world again fore you know it."

Old man Mayfield was eighty-two years old. He was brought to the town of The Walking Wounded when he was twelve years old. He father had just died and his mother was struggling to feed three kids by herself. He loved this place and the people that he called neighbors.

"Before the world was through with us, we'd be just like all the other towns. Full of hate, crime and indifference." Big Red said. "I know what I'm asking you to do is wrong but it's for the right reasons.

"We were all sent here to find a home. If there is anyone who can't go along with this, I can deny any of the charges that the two of them will try to bring against the department. They will have to prove what they are saying. That it's not just their word against ours. But if there is one person, who can't agree with us handling this ourselves, please speak now."

"Are we going to kill them?" A young man asked from the front lawn.

"Yes." Lawrence answered, still not taking his eyes off his shoe.

"Good." The same young man said.

All those sitting on the front lawn nodded approval. Good Lord! We really were in the twilight zone! I thought.

This town reminded me of that town where once a year they had a stoning. It's called The Lottery I believe. Once a year, a name is pulled or a piece of paper is drawn with a black dot on it. If you were the unlucky person, you were literally stoned to death. This town was going to make matters worse by...oh my God!

Two wrongs. They were going to right a wrong with a wrong. I looked at Lawrence.

He was never going to hold his wife again. His son was literally torn from his mother's body. Was it wrong for him to want justice? Was it wrong to want their heads?

I looked at the people sitting on the lawn then I looked back at Lawrence. His attention was still focused on his work boot. I was worried about him. This guy had a whole town backing him. A town that was filled with people that knew pain personally. In fact, it was the common denominator. But Lawrence would have given all of that up to have his wife and son back.

I was left with that thought as the next three days passed by. They were generally uneventful. What made them worth watching at all was that they enforced just how close the people of this town were. It's one thing to mouth the words but actions always speak louder.

And these people' actions said it all. For three days, the whole town basically camped out on the Williams' lawn. The people of this town were at the two family's beck and call. But neither family asked for anything. For the only thing they wanted no one could give them. The towns' people support, love and willingness to help each other made it possible for each of them to get through another day.

During that three-day period, Sidney went with Jake to see the two men who were responsible for taking his little girl away. Blondie stood and went to the bars to face Jake. At one point, he opened his mouth to say something. Big Red pulled his keys and stood ready to open the door. Blondie turned out to be smarter than first believed. For in the end, he said nothing. Goatee laid on his bed with his back to Jake the whole time.

Over the three-day period, many of the towns' people visited the jail. Because the town has never had a prisoner this long, there was not enough staff to cover the three shifts. Many men volunteered to help out. Others simply dropped by to provide food for those that were on watch. The rest stopped by for no other reason than to see those that were responsible for the pain in their lives.

Like Ron Jackson, most of the people wanted to find a monster in those cells. Of course, they didn't. By not finding the boogieman, they were forced to deal with the sad realization that there were people in the world who were capable of that kind of brutality. They were also forced to deal with the fact that those two had some how gotten into their little town. If those two were allowed in, what would keep others from being allowed in?

For three days, I was like Lawrence's shadow. If he went to the bathroom, I went with him. He didn't eat. I didn't want to. His grief was so profound that not only didn't he eat, he didn't sleep or speak. I was worried about him.

I felt his grief. I felt sorrow for him. I think that meant that my heart went out to him but I wasn't sure. I asked Grandma but she didn't answer me. God, I was worried about her too.

Lawrence allowed himself to be hugged and fussed over in those three days but while everyone else's eyes were red and dry or wet and red, his eyes remained dry, clear and focused. Focused on his work boot. During the day, he stared at that boot whether he was wearing it or not.

If he wasn't wearing it, he was carrying it. Needless to say, I wasn't the only one worried. At night, he held that boot to his chest along with one of Bonnie's dolls and he stared at the ceiling. He waited, in that position, for a decent time to get up. The one thing he did not do over those three days was visit the jail.

Originally, I said those three days were not special, just time for me to see a town that was already close grow closer. I was wrong. I learned a lot about how the people interacted with each other. They weren't a bunch of strangers thrown together who had to learn to co-exist. They were a bunch of strangers thrown together who had learned to love each other as a family.

They all had fond memories of Bonnie. The night before the funeral, everyone gathered at the Williams house to share those memories. Lawrence sat staring at his boot as he listened. From time to time, I couldn't help staring at that boot myself.

Mrs. Feldman, the owner of the town's only dry cleaner, told us that Bonnie was tall and clumsy as a child but Lawrence had seen through that awkwardness.

"I remember the day they fell in love. Bonnie's kitten ran into the street. Bless his heart, Lawrence never saw the kitten until it was to late. He must have apologized a hundred times. Bonnie cried. He cried. Out of that kitten's death came their love."

"I remember doing the eulogy for that little kitten." Reverend Martin said. "Lawrence offered to pay me all that he had."

"That couldn't have been much Reverend. He was only thirteen and he was driving on a public street. I might add. All the kids, including Lawrence, knew I didn't care if they drove. Just so long, as it wasn't down town." Big Red said.

"Oh the payment was high Big Red. Because he was paying for disobeying you." Reverend Martin said.

"How much was it Rev.?" Old man Mayfield asked.

"Four dollars and ten cents." We all laughed. Not Lawrence. "But that's not all. He threw in his Babe Ruth baseball card."

"If you'd only known." Sidney said.

"Speaking of driving." Big Red said. "I remember the day you gave Bonnie her first driving lesson." Jake put his head down and shook it. He laughed before he spoke.

"Boy was that a nightmare."

"I don't think anyone has ever been as happy to see me Jake as you were."

"Little good it did. You walked up, looked at me then her. She was already nervous. You pulling us over didn't help. But she smiled at you and my hopes of getting out of the rest of that lesson went out the window. Remember what you said to her."

"Yeah. I told her not to drive with both feet." Everyone laughed at that.

"Oh yeah. You were a big help that day Red."

"She smiled at me. What else could I do?"

What else indeed? I too had been a recipient of that smile. Everyone got quiet as they remembered her. Not for long though. There were many stories to be told. Remembering the happy times help wash away some of the fear and the pain everyone had been feeling.

That time was therapeutic for everyone involved even me. I didn't know Bonnie in life. My time with her had been brief and terrifying. Learning about her and the people of this town made me understand what Grandma had tried to explain to me. These people were more alive than any group of people I knew. They haven't always been that way. Except for those born here, they were all like me. I was a Walking Wounded.

On the day of the funeral, Lawrence and I were up and dressed at six a.m. He put on a pair of dress shoes. Today, instead of carrying one work boot, he carried them both. At the gravesite, he placed those boots at the bottom of the grave. Before the casket containing his wife and child was lowered, he placed two red roses on top. Then he walked away.

"Jake go with him." Tina said.

"No honey. Let him have this time."

"But I'm worried about him." Sarah said.

"So are we. But I think Jake's right." Sidney said.

"God please be with him." Reverend Martin prayed and the whole town said Amen.

Lawrence and I walked about a mile and a half through the woods directly behind the church. It should have been a very peaceful walk but for some reason I was unnerved. Like Sarah and Tina, I feared he had plans of hurting himself.

When he sat down on an old tree stump, I decided three days was long enough to be quiet. I stood looking down at him, trying to find a way to say what I was feeling. In the end, I just opened my mouth.

"She was looking forward to telling you how her doctor's visit had gone. She'd planned a special dinner for you." I stopped and waited. Lawrence didn't move or say anything. He just twirled a blade of grass between his fingers.

"She was very brave. She did what they told her to do. She gave them all the money she had. Still it wasn't what they wanted. They knew by the car she was driving they wouldn't get much money. But she did everything she was told to do.

"Her main concern was the baby. It wasn't until she realized that they were going to hurt him that she fought them with everything she had. I'm convinced she would have won had there only been one of them. I'm convinced of that."

Lawrence stopped twirling that blade of grass. In fact, he dropped it. And as if he were in some kind of time warp, he slowly looked at me.

I took a step back. Like Bonnie, he could see me. He could hear me. With large sad blue eyes, he stared at me. They were the same blue eyes that Bonnie had looked into. I saw no love in those eyes. I saw no tears in those eyes. I saw only pain.

"She could see me too." I said sitting beside him. "She thought I was an angel sent to help her."

"Are you?"

"No."

"Did you? Help her I mean."

"I couldn't save her. I held her hand and covered her eyes. I kept your son breathing until she got to him. I helped her lift him so that she could hold him before she died. She got to kiss and console him. I know that doesn't sound like enough but it was all that I could do."

"Then it was enough. Thank you."

"How can you say that?" I yelled. "I wanted to rip their hearts out but I couldn't even touch them!"

"I can. I wasn't sent here." He said, then he stood. So did I.

"I'm sorry Lawrence. I really am. I knew before I met her she was going to die. I thought I was sent to change that, to make a difference. But I wasn't and I couldn't." I said kicking the old stump.

Lawrence turned his back to me. He started to take a step forward then stopped. He reached into his pocket for something then turned back to me. When he removed his hand, he was holding a gun.

"Jesus Christ Lawrence where did you get that?"

"I've known about you for the last three days."

"Lawrence answer me! Where did you get that thing?"

"What's your name?" When I didn't answer he spoke again. "You know my name."

"Matty. I'm sorry. I should have introduced myself."

"Short for Matthew?" I nodded.

"Jake bought this thing twenty-three years ago. Before moving here. When Bonnie was born, he put it in a shoebox and hid it. His intentions were to get rid of it. Until three days ago, he all but forgot he'd ever owned a gun.

"The day he went to see the animals that killed Bonnie he remembered it and unearthed it. He wanted to shoot them but Tina prevailed upon him to let Big Red handle them. I took it this morning." He looked at me. "Maybe you have made a difference Matty."

He held the gun out to me. I hesitated only for a moment then I held my hand out. I emptied the gun then threw it as far away as I could.

"What will you do?" He shrugged then walked away. To walk beside him I had to run and catch up.

Two miles later we came out into a clearing. We were two houses away from his own home. As before, there was a large crowd waiting on his lawn.

"Why are all those people there?"

"Like you, they feared I would commit suicide. I guess they figured if I didn't, I would eventually show up here." I nodded and followed him as he started home.

"There he is!" We heard old man Mayfield say. I watched as all heads turned to find Lawrence. From twenty feet way, we could hear them sigh.

"Thank God!" Sidney said hugging his son when they were close enough. "We were so worried about you."

"Honey why don't you come with us back to Tina's and Jake's. You haven't eaten in three days. There's a ton of food there. All your favorites." Sarah said.

She was never so happy to see her son as she was right now. But she couldn't help feeling a little guilty. Lawrence was hurting but he was alive. She wished Bonnie were too. Not just for Lawrence but for Jake and Tina.

"I don't want to eat right now. I have some things to do first."

"Like what?" Jake asked.

Lawrence didn't answer. Instead, he pulled away from both sets of parents and went to his garage. There, he stood in front of two gas cans. The first one he picked up was full. The second one sounded to be about half full maybe more. He took the full can and tilted it forward spilling gasoline as he went.

Jake took the other can and did the same. From the kitchen Jake went through the living room down the hall until he was out of site. Lawrence went through the living room and out the front door. He circled his house saturating the outside while Jake saturated the inside. They joined each other on the front porch when their can was empty.

"Anymore in that can." Jake asked.

"No. Empty."

"We'll need more." Jake said.

"Give me those cans." Old man Mayfield said. "I have a full tank. I'll siphon you some."

"Thanks. We really need a good soaking."

Jake and Lawrence stood on the porch looking at the crowd. Initially, everyone was surprised. It didn't take long to understand the rational though. Everyone watched quietly. Old man Mayfield started down the steps. At the bottom, Sidney, who was holding a small bucket, stopped him. In that bucket was more gasoline.

"If this is what the two of you want to do at least let me help." He said.

"What else is there to do Sidney? There's no way he'll ever be able to live in this house. There's no way Tina and I will ever be able to visit here again. The best thing to do is burn it down."

"I agree Jake. So does this whole town. I don't think there's anyone in this town that hasn't been in this house at least once. I'm sure no one in this town will ever be able to walk through those doors without remembering. Hell Jake, we're gonna remember whether this house is here or not. But I'm worried about Lawrence waking up tomorrow with regrets."

Jake thought about that for a moment then nodded. "He's right son." Jake said looking at Lawrence.

Instead of answering either his father or his father in law, he walked down the steps, took the bucket of gas then turned to old man Mayfield.

"Mr. Mayfield can I still have that gas?"

"You bet you can son." Old man Mayfield said then looked at Sidney, who patted him on the back before stepping aside.

At old man Mayfield's truck, three young men stood ready to help. One provided a hose; another took the can, while the other went to work retrieving the gas.

Lawrence used the gas he got from his father inside the house. He poured most of it on the carpet. The rest he poured on the over turned sofa and chair. Jake, Sidney, Tina, Sarah and I stood at the door. Neither of us spoke. Besides, what was there to say?

While we watched, Lawrence turned the gas can upside down to make sure all of its contents were gone. Empty. He threw it in a corner.

"I'm done in here." He told us.

"What about some clothes Lawrence?" I asked. You've got to have something else to wear besides your suite.

He looked at me blankly for a moment then at himself. "Wait." He said, then he disappeared into the bedroom. When he returned, he was wearing a green tee shirt and a pair of jeans.

"Maybe you ought to change your shoes too. Those have gas all over them." I suggested. He looked at his feet then disappeared again.

Jake and Sidney looked at each other. When Lawrence returned, he was carrying a pair of sneakers. Like Goatee and Blondie's shoes they were converses. I guess that must have been the shoe of this time.

At the door, Lawrence looked at me. "Don't you want a picture or something?"

He looked back then slowly shook his head. Not understanding, Jake and Sidney looked at each other again.

"Are you alright son?" Sidney asked.

"No dad. I can't say that I am."

"Lawrence you don't have to do this today. Why don't you take sometime to think about this for a while longer?"

"Time won't bring them back."

"Where will you live?" Lawrence looked into his father's eyes.

"Are you saying I can't live with you and mom until I figure things out?"

"No that's not what I'm saying. You're always welcome. I'm just worried you're making a mistake."

"I'm not."

"Honey take something with you. You're not even taking anything to remember her by?" Sarah said.

"All I need to remember her by is right up here." He said tapping his head. "Besides, all I ever wanted is already gone." At that he waved us to back away. Lawrence went to Old man Mayfield, who was waiting on the steps for him.

"Got enough." Mrs. Feldman asked after Lawrence splashed the sides of the house.

"I think so."

Lawrence pulled one shoe from his right pocket and put it on then repeated the act with the left shoe. When he had both dress shoes off, he threw them on the front porch. To make sure he was safe, he lit a match then threw it at the trail of gas that he had carried only about half way down the driveway.

We all watched as the flames licked it's way up the driveway, up the steps and into the house. Whoosh! The living room started to burn. Lawrence threw another match along side the house. In no time, a circle of flames surrounded it. Lawrence then sat on the grass to watch.

"Who are they Big Red?" Lawrence asked.

"I don't know. Haven't bothered to ask." He looked at Lawrence. "Does it matter?"

"No. It doesn't." Big Red nodded then looked back at the burning house.

I thought of the camping trips I shared with my father. We would always build a fire then sit and watch it for hours. This would have been a great bonfire had the house not been such a grim reminder.

"Lawrence, see that woman over there." I said pointing. "That's who sent me here." He asked why with his head and his eyes. He knew he couldn't ask me with his mouth.

"Because she wanted to help me. See she knew I was hurting even when I didn't. For the last sixteen years, I've been running from my past. I didn't care about anyone and I made it impossible for anyone to care about me. I'm twenty-five years from the future."

He looked at me with a lot of doubt in his eyes. In the end, he shrugged telling me he believed me.

"I didn't want to be here at first. I have to admit I've seen more than I could have ever bargained for and I've learned more than I could have ever hoped for. I just wished you hadn't lost your family. I wish I could have been more helpful. I wish…"

Lawrence put his hand up to his eyes and I shut up. When he looked up again, his eyes were still dry. I changed the subject anyway. "By the time I meet you, you'll be fifty-nine years old. See Grandma is going to send me here to live."

Lawrence looked at me for a moment then looked away. Initially, I took that as a bad sign. Like maybe he didn't want me here. I felt sad and hurt. If he didn't want me here, why would any of his neighbors want me? I started to turn away when I noticed his arm was shaking. Upon closer inspection, I realized that he was giving me the thumbs up sign.

"Thanks." I said smiling and feeling relieved. He answered me by ever so quickly nodding his head. Then he turned to Big Red.

"I know how I want to handle this." E.F. Hutton might as well have spoken.

The effect was the same. Once he had everyone's attention, he didn't say anything else. Instead, he pulled a blade of grass from the ground and placed it in his mouth.

"Don't make me guess son. How do you want to handle them?" Big Red asked.

"I want to take each one of them on." He paused for a response. When he didn't get one, he went on. "If either one of them or both of them can beat me, they walk."

"What are the chances of that happening?" Big Red asked.

"I have good reason to believe that Bonnie would still be alive if she hadn't been double teamed. So I'm going to do what my wife couldn't do."

"How do you know that?" Jake asked. "One of them has a black eye; the other has a swollen nose. Both are signs my baby put up a fight. But those injuries are a long way from…from winning." Lawrence looked at me.

"She kicked both of them in the balls. It's just that when one was down the other was recovered." I told him. He smiled. It was the first smile that I'd seen from him.

"Let's just say, I bet, neither of them are crossing their legs right about now."

"Okay. I can believe and live with that." Jake said slowly.

"How about it Big Red?" Lawrence asked.

"I'll set it up."

"For tonight." Lawrence said. That request received the first negative reaction I'd heard since being here.

"No way son." Sidney said.

"Listen to your father Lawrence. He's right." Big Red said. "You haven't eaten or slept in three days. I'll set it up, just not for tonight."

"Tonight Big Red. I'm as ready as I'm ever going to get. Food and sleep won't change that!"

"Like hell it won't!" Jake said. "It'll build your strength up."

"Set it up for tonight please. I'm ready." Lawrence repeated. The crowd voiced their disapproval. "I'm ready! I tell you!" He yelled looking around.

"Lawrence you're tying our hands. If for some reason you lose and one, just one of them beat you, according to your own rules, there is nothing we'll be able to do about it." Big Red said trying to reason with him.

"Big Red do you know why I had to look in the kitchen three days ago? Do you know why I had to see what they had done to my wife and to our child? Do you know why?" The crowd grew quiet. Big Red looked away.

" I did promise you, you could deal with them anyway you saw fit. I'm not going back on that. I just wish you wouldn't do it tonight."

"This town has always believed in me. Don't stop now. I've never let anyone down before. I won't start now. I owe this to my family. I owe it to myself.

"I need to do this for my future. I'm going to have to live without the only woman I've ever loved. I don't have a choice there but if I'm going to kill two men and I am going to kill them then I need to be able to live with myself. The only way for me to do that is to know I gave them a fair chance."

Initially Big Red made no response. The crowd was quiet. The only thing that could be heard was the sound the flames made as they steadily consumed the house.

"I'll set it up for dark." Big Red said. This answer made everyone happy. To prove it, the crowd clapped and cheered.

"Bonnie would be proud of you son but you don't have to do this by yourself. I could…"

"Yes I do!" Lawrence said quickly. "I do have to do this myself."

"Lawrence…"

"Jake you still have Tina. Dad has mom. When things settle down, the four of you will go on with your lives together. Eventually, I'll go on with my life.

"The difference is I won't have anyone to share it with. My anniversary will be spent alone. Same thing with holidays. I'm the one who won't have anyone to tell how my day went. I'm the one who will be sleeping alone. So you see, I have to do this my way."

"Yes, I guess you do." Jake said putting his arms around Lawrence. They hugged tightly then they looked at each other. "You know I tried to see things through your eyes. I didn't like what I saw.

"You're right, I still have Tina. If anything were to ever happen to her, I think I'd lose my mind. I'd…"

"You'd want to kill someone with your bare hands?" Lawrence finished for him. Jake nodded. "And you dad." Sidney also nodded. He took Sarah's hand in his own.

"How can we help you Big Red?" Jake asked after looking at Tina. He took her hand and kissed it.

"We need a place to meet." He said.

"How bout my place?" Old man Mayfield said. "It's far enough away from prying eyes." That suggestion was met with approval.

Big Red should have been surprised by the town's support but he wasn't. He knew his people well. He knew, as a rule, his people had been through some horrendous circumstances. Most of them had to deal with them alone.

All that changed when they arrived in the town of The Walking Wounded. Help is just a request away, in any direction. Now was no exception.

"I'll also need some able bodied men to form a circle."

There are only three hundred and seventy-five people residing in this town. One hundred and forty-eight of them are men. All one hundred and forty-eight considered themselves to be able-bodied including old man Mayfield. I laughed at their confidence. Lawrence looked at me and smiled.

"Thank you. All of you. But I don't need a circle that big." Lawrence said. "I don't want to run them to death." At that, everyone laughed, including Lawrence. "I think I'm gonna check around back to make sure the flames haven't jumped. Lawrence said excusing himself.

He knew Big Red was going to have to eliminate a lot of men. He knew it was going to be a difficult task. He appreciated that but he didn't want to watch it.

Once out of site he turned to me. "So Matty, what's it like in the future?"

"Not as good as you have it here." I told him.

"You mean in twenty-five years there is still racial tension and world conflict?" He asked looking at me. A frown knitted his brow together.

"Yes. That and a whole lot of other problems. They aren't as blatant as they used to be but the KKK still exists. There are a few other groups that were formed for the soul purpose of spreading hate. A lot of laws have been passed. Schools and jobs are integrated. But in twenty-five years, the world is no where close to having what this town has."

"Thanks. I was hoping I'd have something to live for. Something to look forward to."

"You do Lawrence. With time, this pain will get better. It may never go away totally but it'll get better. How can it not get better? Look at what you have got here. I've never seen a support group as big as this one. These people love you."

"I know. Believe me Matty, I really do. But do you know what I'd give to be able to make love to my wife right now? Do you know what I'd give to just hold her?" I shook my head.

"I'd give my soul. If God would let me hold her just one more time, I'd die in her place. I'd do anything to bring her back just so that I could say goodbye. I didn't even get to say goodbye." He said.

For a moment, I thought he was going to cry. His eyes got wet but he fought hard to keep those tears from spilling and they didn't.

"Why won't you cry Lawrence?"

"I can't. Every time I get the urge to cry, I think of those two sonsofbitches in that jail. All I get is angry. There'll be time for crying when I have dealt with them."

At that, he turned and went back to the front of the house. On the way around, we ran into Big Red, who was coming to find us.

"Got everything set up. I'm gonna go over and give those two the verdict." He said patting Lawrence on the back. "Got to give it to you son. You're a better man than I am. I think I would have shot them both on site."

"I don't believe that Big Red."

"You don't huh? I think you and the rest of the people in this town forget I'm just a man."

"Grace called you Big Red. You were the second person to know that Bonnie had met with foul play at their hand. You had them and you didn't shoot them. I think we know exactly who you are."

Big Red thought about that for a moment then he extended his hand. Lawrence held his out. They shook then they hugged.

"God I hope you're right." He said.

"I hope you never have to find out." Big Red nodded then turned to leave. I followed.

I got in the car with him and rode to the jail. Waiting for him outside of the jail was the rest of his crew.

"You think he can beat them both?" Paul asked.

"Under the circumstances couldn't you?" Ron Jackson asked. "I'd beat them both or die knowing that I'd given it my best."

"Me too." Carl said. "What about you Big Red? What would you do?"

"I'd like to think I'd be as fair as Lawrence but I think I would just put a bullet through the center of each of their heads."

"A man has to do what a man has to do." Ronnie said. "But I don't think you would be among us now Big Red if you could do that. Like the rest of us, you're hurt and angry but you're not capable of that kind of brutality. If you were, you would have shot them when you had the chance."

"That's the same thing Lawrence said to me." Big Red said then ran his hand over his chin. He took a moment to think then looked back at his men. He turned to Paul and answered the original question. "He has what it takes to beat them. He has what it takes and then some."

When we walked inside, Goatee didn't move. Blondie, on the other hand, got up and came to the bars. "What does a person have to do to get some food around here?" He asked.

"The town has come to a verdict." Big Red said ignoring Blondie.

There were two desks present in the main office. Big Red sat on the front of the one off to the right of the door. Ronnie sat behind the same desk. Jackson sat on the front of the desk on the left. Carl sat behind it. Paul stood in the doorway. As did I.

"What do you mean the verdict?" Blondie asked. He placed both hands on the bars. "We haven't seen no lawyer. We haven't seen no judge. Hell, we haven't seen nothing but the inside of these cells for three days."

"Gonna change that for you boy. Tonight, we're gonna take you boys for a ride. Tonight, we're gonna introduce you to that little gal's husband. One by one.

Either or both of you can beat him, you get to walk away from this with nothing more than the bruises that you get. Does that sound fair enough to you boys?" The room was so quiet only the hum of electricity could be heard.

"What's the catch?" Blondie asked. Goatee was up now and looking at us with the same question on his face but not speaking it.

"No catch."

"What if we refuse?" Goatee asked. All eyes turned towards him, no one had heard him speak since the arrest.

"You don't have a choice. You're getting in the ring with Lawrence Phillips. You choose not to fight he's going to kick your brains in anyway. See boys, he buried his family today. You're the reason for his misery." Ron Jackson answered.

"There are always choices." Blondie said.

"Yeah, like the choice you gave Bonnie and her son?" Big Red asked. "You'll meet in the ring after dark. The entire town will be present to make sure you don't try to get away."

"What kinda weapon will he have?" Blondie asked.

"Just his fist. If he was going to be using a weapon, he wouldn't be in a ring with you?" Paul pointed out.

"So then he must be a black belt or something."

"Wrong again Einstein." Paul said, then he turned to Big Red. "I've thought about what you said Big Red and I have to agree with you. I'd just shoot em." Big Red nodded.

"There is one condition." Big Red said. "Try to run and all bets are off."

"You're serious, aren't you?" Goatee asked. "There is no catch."

"That's right."

"What's to stop us from coming back here and blowing this town off the map later?" Blondie asked.

"Nothing. But if you come back, you'll have to deal with us. We'll shoot you on sight."

"Crazy. This whole town is crazy." Blondie said.

"We're crazy? You raped and beat a pregnant lady! You cut her baby from her body. You watched her crawl across the floor to her baby then you watched them both die and you call us..."

"She died first." Blondie said proud of himself.

All the officers looked at each other. The room was quiet again. Ron's heart was beating so loud I could hear it from where I was standing. All of them had to fight the urge to draw their gun and open fire. It was the most hate either of them had ever felt.

"You know what Big Red? Why don't we open the cells and let them go. We could go over and tell Lawrence that bit of news. Then we could tell him and the rest of the folks that it's a free for all." Ronnie suggested when he realized he couldn't shoot an unarmed man even if that man was an animal.

"I would love too. But then we wouldn't be any better than them. Plus we gave Lawrence our word." Big Red turned to Ron. "Still think I would be wrong to put a bullet through each of their heads?" Ron shook his head then stood and headed for the door. They all left. I wanted to go too but I didn't. It wasn't time for me to go.

"Hey man you're not worried are you?" Blondie asked

"Aren't you?"

"Hell no! You heard them. He ain't got no black belt or nothing. I have a black belt. Remember? I'll kill him."

"Good. You can go first." Goatee said remembering but not comforted by the knowledge.

"Okay. But you owe me one when this is over."

"Man we get out of this alive; you can have anything you want." That was what I was to hear. Afterwards, I was allowed to leave.

In a blink, I found myself standing next to Lawrence. We were back in the cemetery.

"Where were you Matty?"

"The jail." I told him. "The blond one knows karate."

"It'll take more than that."

I looked at him. He wasn't bragging just stating his feeling. He knelt beside Bonnie's grave. He held a rose in his hand and from time to time he swirled it around between his fingers. He plucked a petal then let it fall on top of her grave.

"Why are you here?" I asked. "Shouldn't you be preparing yourself for the fight?

"Prepared. Besides, I have nowhere else to go. My family's here."

"Yeah but you can't live here. You can't…" He spun around to look at me. This caused me to stop and start over. "Lawrence this part of your life is over. I know you'll never forget them but you can't stay here."

"Do you believe in God?" He looked away then dropped another petal. When I didn't answer him, he asked me another question. "Why do you think God let this happen?"

"I don't know. Grandma said ours was not to question why? I don't think I will go through life never wondering from time to time but that's what she told me when I asked her why God let my father die and why he let my step father assault me."

"I know why." He said, letting another petal fall. "He's testing me. I'm Job and he's testing me."

"Why?"

"For the same reason."

"Oh." I said watching the petal as it fell. I was ashamed of myself for not knowing what he was talking about. I was even more ashamed for not asking him to explain. "Have you passed this test?" I asked.

"No. I can't pass it. But I'm trying to be as fair as possible. I'm giving them a fair chance. That's more than they gave Bonnie. That's the best I can do."

"Grandma asked me if two wrongs made a right. What do you think?"

"Of course it doesn't! That's why I'm failing the test. Two wrongs never make a right. But I'm only human.

"I don't think the justice system will sufficiently punish them for what they did. I can't even be sure they won't be back on the street within the year. For that reason, I have asked the people of this town to support me."

"No you didn't."

"Yes. I did."

"I've watched the people of this town. They wanted Big Red to hold those two for you, long before you even cleared your head enough to decide what you wanted to do. Those people want to see justice too. Believe me, you're not asking them to do anything they don't want."

"Thanks. That helps." He let another petal fall and we both watched in silence as it drifted to the ground. "She loves me." He said as it hit the ground. It was the last petal. He smiled.

"I've always known that." He stood. "That's why I have to do this. But tell Grandma the answer is no. Do as I say not as I do. Okay?"

"What if…"

"No what ifs! Just tell her no!" He said turning so that he could yell right into my face.

When I nodded, he turned and walked away. I followed. Periodically I looked at him. Neither of us spoke as we walked away from town.

He walked with his head down watching his feet. The moon was full and although it provided us with enough light, I didn't like being in the middle of nowhere in the dark. After about a mile, I noticed movement ahead of us.

We had arrived at the Mayfield farm. The lawn of people had moved from Lawrence's house to here and we were headed straight for them. Lawrence and I joined his father and Jake. They were sitting around yet another fire. At least, this time it wasn't a house burning.

Big Red brought Blondie and Goatee, as he'd promised. At the moment, they were locked in the backseat of his black and white. They were watching and enjoying the fire as if they had been invited as guest. For the moment, they were being ignored.

I watched as the flames licked around a log that it was in the process of consuming. I looked around me. There were many small groups all trying to forget the tragedy that had visited them. I decided to enjoy the fire too. No one seemed to be in any hurry. The only two that may have been ready to get things started were Blondie and Goatee.

I kicked at a log that was half out of the fire. When it didn't move, Lawrence kicked at it. He caused the whole structure to collapse. When it did, the sweet music of wood crackling could be heard everywhere. The scent of burning pine filled the air. It was a great scene except for the pain that surrounded me.

For three days, I've been by Lawrence's side for almost every move he's made. He's known I was here for those three days but it wasn't until today that he acknowledged my presence. He even gave me advice. He advised me to tell Grandma two wrongs didn't make a right. Still, I found it hard not to believe in what he was doing.

Lawrence watched as the flames danced in the pit. His eyes lit up as if they were flames too. After a moment, he stood, brushed the dirt off his pants then rubbed his hands together before speaking.

"I'm ready Big Red."

"All right men, let's form that circle." Big Red had chosen his circle well. It consisted of every deputy and every acting deputy. While the circle was forming, Big Red went to the black and white.

"Which one of you want to go first?"

"Yours truly." Blondie said. He got out and smiled at Goatee through the window before going with Big Red.

"See you in a minute." He said. Big Red smiled too.

"I'll say one thing for you boy. You got balls. I guess that's good since you ain't got brains." Blondie rolled his eyes but he didn't say anything.

As they approached, the circle opened so that Blondie could step in. It closed with Big Red being the finial link.

Goatee watched as the circle closed behind his best friend. Big Red had parked the car on a hill so that whoever was last could watch the fight without being hindered by anything. Goatee watched as his best friend faced Lawrence. He watched as Blondie assumed the familiar karate position.

Lawrence looked at Blondie and did not see a man, someone's best friend or otherwise. All he saw was the reason for his loneliness, pain, anger and hurt. He moved into Blondie's space and stance so fast that he never saw him coming. He caught Blondie with a fist to his chest then to his face.

He pounded and pounded Blondie until Blondie gave up trying karate and resorted to street fighting. Blondie tried to match punch for punch. He failed. In the end, Goatee watched as Lawrence defeated his best friend and his only hope in less than ten minutes.

Johnny Stevens pulled Lawrence away so that he could check for a pulse. Finding none, he called for one of the two stretchers that he had provided. With Blondie's body out of the way, Big Red went for Goatee. When he motioned for him to get out, Goatee refused.

"Shoes on the other foot and you don't like it do you? You chicken shit!" Old man Mayfield yelled.

"Be a man. Fight like a man. At least go out like a man." Frank Stanton yelled.

"Chicken shit." Old man Mayfield yelled again.

I looked at that old man. He loved his neighbors and I knew why. When his Nancy was in bed after having her first stroke, every woman in town signed up to take care of her. Many husbands accompanied their wives. Lawrence and Bonnie always went together.

"I told you, you couldn't refuse. Now get out of the car or I'll have to pull you out. I wouldn't want to ruin your chances by hurting you. So my advice to you is to get out on your own. Now get out!" Goatee did as he was told. As with Blondie, the circle opened then closed around him.

Goatee did not assume any kind of karate stance. He didn't ball his fist. Instead, he looked at Blondie's body then turned and ran. Joined hands locked the circle. He ran into the hands of Ronnie and Carl. Their hands didn't break and this reminded me of a game I played at camp.

Red rover, red rover send Goatee right over. I half expected them to let him become part of the circle when he couldn't break it. Instead, Ronnie and Carl simply pushed him back towards the center and Lawrence. Goatee looked around him. Turning around slowly, he finally faced Lawrence. Tentatively, he stepped forward.

"Lawrence wait!" Lawrence looked at him but didn't speak. "I want to ask for mercy. I know what we did hurt a lot of people but this isn't going to bring either of them back. I'm sorry. I'm really sorry."

"What's your name?"

"Tony."

"Did my wife beg you for mercy Tony?" Tony dropped his head and nodded. "And I'm sure she begged you to spare our son's life, didn't she?" Again he nodded yes.

"You know my wife and I could have dealt with the two of you raping her. We wouldn't have liked it but we were strong. We would have got past it. But you didn't stop there.

"Hell, the two of you probably laughed at her. So here's the deal. I'm giving you a chance Tony. That's more than you gave her. That's the best I can do." Lawrence said. Then he wiped his nose and mouth. Both were bleeding.

His clothes were dirt stained and bloody. His hair stood up all over his head. His eyes still glowed like fire. In a word he looked like an escaped psycho.

"What if I don't fight you?"

"Then you die without even trying."

"Is that what your wife would have wanted?" Tony asked tears running down his face.

"You didn't know my wife." Lawrence yelled charging Goatee. "You didn't know her." He yelled over and over again as he pounded his fist into Goatee. "You didn't know her." He was still yelling a few minutes later when Jake and Sidney pulled him off Goatee's inert body.

"Don't ask me to be a bigger man, a better man than you. I can't do it! I can't do it!" He yelled.

Lawrence's voice was full of rage, despair, loneliness and hurt. He looked at Jake then Sidney. "I can't do it." He sobbed. They knelt beside him on the ground. Johnny motion to have Goatee's body removed.

Lawrence remained on his knees breathing heavy. When the two bodies were placed side by side, he looked at his hands. Still over whelmed by despair and anger, he leaned forward and bowed.

In that position, he pounded the ground as he had pounded Blondie and Goatee's bodies. The difference is that this time he was able to cry.

Jake and Sidney stayed by his side and cried as well. I looked around and found everyone was crying. Sarah and Tina joined the three men and held them.

Their neighbors one by one joined them as well. Each one adding to the hug. In the end, I joined the circle of people and cried too.

When I realized I was no longer a part of the circle, I looked up. I was surprised and relieved to find that I was back in Grandma's room. Her face was wet. Her eyes still closed.

I looked at the monitor. Her rate was thirty. Her skin was cold and clammy. I touched her gently, trying to get her attention. It was five fifteen. I didn't think she would live to see five thirty.

"Grandma?" I asked sitting on the bed and taking her hand.

"I'm still here." She whispered. Then she coughed.

Her lungs were so congested she was literally drowning. Why hadn't Sadie Poole treated her? Why wasn't any one taking care of her? I headed for the door to find answers to my questions. But her soft voice stopped me.

"I'm not long of this world now Matty. I must have an answer." I sat on the edge of the bed and took her hand in my own.

"His punishment was fair. He…they killed his family." I stopped then sighed. "I'd be lying to you if I told you I didn't think he was justified. I don't think I would have even given them the benefit of doubt." I turned away. I knew I had failed.

She sighed then coughed again. "The question wasn't whether or not he was justified. "The question." She stopped to catch her breath. She was wheezing and her breath was so short I tried to make her hush. I wanted her to save all her energy for breathing. "Does two wrongs make a right Matty?"

"No Grandma. No it does not. Two wrongs do not make a right. Look let me get the crash cart and some Lasix. I can help you. I can make it easier for you to breathe."

"Don't bother child. These old bones are tired. They need to rest. Don't you fret none. I'll be in good hands when I leave yours." She said smiling. "Lean closer child. I have some directions for you."

"Was that real? I mean did that really happen?"

"Just tell them Grandma sent ya. Okay?" The alarms went off again when her heart rate dropped to twenty-eight.

"Are you hurting?" I asked positioning myself so that I could pull her into my arms.

"No."

"Isn't there something I can do for you Grandma?"

"You already are Matty. You already are." She said then sighed one last time. I stayed with her long after the monitor read zero. I cried as if I'd know her all my life.

The tears made me feel better. They made me feel clean somehow. I closed my eyes to pray.

When I opened my eyes again, it was to the sound of my beeper going off. I was in the call room still undressed. By the looks of things, I'd been there all night. I looked at my watch. Five fifteen.

Five fifteen, why did that seem familiar? I dialed the number to the unit. All the while wondering why I felt so un-rested. I wondered why my eyes were burning and why my nose was congested. The only thing I could figure was that I was allergic to something used to do the laundry.

"This is Dr Green."

"Good morning Dr Green this is Sadie. Have you had time to view any of the labs?"

"Not yet. What's up?"

"Mrs. Smith's mag and potassium are low and she doesn't have an order to cover that."

"Okay." I said. "I'll be right there. Oh Sadie. Can you tell me how Mrs. Morris is doing?"

"Wrong unit doc. We don't have a Morris."

"Oh. Okay. My mistake, I'm sorry."

"No problem doc."

"What the…?" Had last night been a dream? Had I been so uptight about being on call last night that I made things worse than they really were? I got up, went to the computer and typed in the name of Ruthie Mae Morris.

There were three entries in the computer. Neither of them was the one I wanted. What was going on? I know I admitted a Ruthie Mae Morris last night. Yet she didn't show up in the computer. I tried to remember her social security number but couldn't. I looked through my index cards. There was not one for her because there was no Grandma Morris.

With my sanity hanging by a thread, I got dressed and went to the unit. This time of the morning was busy and I was able to walk in unnoticed. Something about being here unnoticed felt familiar too. I went straight to room six and looked in.

It was empty. The bed was made. The room was clean. The monitor was off. There was only one sign that I'd been in this room. The clock on the wall was stuck at five fifteen. The problem is I didn't know if that was a.m. or p.m. I was more confused than before.

I walked out of room six. No one noticed me as I sat down at the nurse's station. For no reason that I could think of, I picked up the phone. Who was I calling and why? I dialed a number I didn't know then I waited for an answer.

"Hello." The voice belonged to a female. Like everything else, it was familiar. "Hello is anyone there?"

Then it hit me. I opened my mouth to speak but no words came out. The voice belonged to my sister. Without speaking, I hung up. There had been a Ruthie Mae Morris. I can't explain how I know, I just know.

I stood and walked back into room six. There, I took my badge, my beeper and my lab jacket off. I placed them on the bed. When Sadie Poole walked in to see what I was doing, I walked out.

"Dr. Green is everything all right?" She asked. I didn't answer.

With both hands, I opened the door to the unit and walked out. At the elevator, I waited alone. When the doors opened, I got in an empty box. When the doors opened again two floors from where I started, I found myself staring at Dr Charlesdale and Dr. Jean Woods.

I looked first at Jean then Dr Charlesdale but spoke to neither. The running joke around the hospital is that if you are an intern Dr Charlesdale didn't acknowledge you until you spoke to him first. That was okay with me, I didn't care to be acknowledged today.

I pushed past both of them and headed for the nearest exit. "And just where do you think you're going Dr Green?" Dr Charlesdale asked my back.

I didn't answer him. I just kept walking. I knew without looking back at him, his face was slowly flushing with anger.

Without looking, I knew he and Jean looked at each other then turned to follow me. Their footsteps started out slow at first then they increased to a rapid pace in an attempt to catch up with me.

"Dr Green! Matthew!" Jean yelled following me. I turned to face them only after I'd gotten to my car and opened the door.

"Is there something you need to tell me Dr Green?" Dr Charlesdale asked.

"Yeah there is. I'm leaving."

"Now would you like to tell me why?"

"No." I got in my car.

"Dr Green, before you throw away years of hard work, let's talk about this."

"I can't. I have a date." I closed the door, started the car then drove away. I had no clue where I was going and I wasn't sure I knew who I was going to see.

My car seemed to know. Four hours later, at a quarter of ten, I pulled into another parking lot. The building was a newly built CVS drug store. I stepped into the store, looked around and immediately knew why I'd been brought here.

The girl behind the counter was six years older, a lot skinnier and not nearly as pretty as I remembered. Her hair was pulled back into a ponytail, which only made the angles of her face too sharp. She wore too much makeup and when she smiled she seemed to wince. Like maybe smiling made her face hurt.

Her eyes were dull. Her voice was soft. When her last customer walked away, I stepped to the counter. A closer inspection showed me that maybe it did hurt for her to smile. We looked at each other without speaking.

My sister was another member of The Walking Wounded club. The right side of her face was puffy. The ton of makeup she'd applied wasn't working that well at hiding her black eye.

At first, her dull gray eyes grew duller then a small light went on and she realized the guy standing and staring at her was her baby brother.

"Mat? Matty is that you?"

"Yeah." Her smile made the swelling look worse. "It's me."

When we were growing up, I always thought my sister was prettier than any of my friend's sisters. I still did. But I was looking at her with my heart now and not my eyes. Because if the truth were told, the last eight years had not been kind to her.

Her smile had not changed. It was the same as when we were kids. It transformed her somehow to a time before the black eyes.

"Chris I want you to come with me."

"Where?"

"I don't know. I just know that it's better than what either of us have right now. I know that you'll never have to cover another one of those up again." I said pointing at her eye. She dropped her head.

"Matty I can't go with you. You don't even know where you're going for crying out loud." That was Chris, always practical.

"Chris I need for you to come with me. I need for you to trust me."

"I really need this job Matty."

"You'll be able to find another one. I promise."

"Trust you. You promise. Matty I haven't seen you…"

"Not here. Let's talk about this on the way. Come on." She didn't move. She just stood staring at me. "Chris I know I haven't been there for you. But I'm about to make that up to you. If you'll just let me. Please come with me." I said holding my hand out to her.

She looked at it. She looked around the store then she looked at my hand again. Finally, she nodded then reached for it.

That's the last thing I remember until six twenty-five p.m. At which time, I found myself pulling into yet another parking lot. I looked over at Chris. She had slept most of the trip and was asleep now.

I think at some point, maybe, I had been asleep too. I sat behind the wheel but the car drove itself. I thought about a movie I had watched a while back where something like that really happened. I reached over to wake Chris.

"Chris." I said shaking her leg. "We're here." She blinked, looked around then looked at me.

"Where's here?"

"I don't know." I said opening my door.

Chris looked at me with questions in her eyes. She didn't say anything she simply trusted me and opened her door. I waited for her at the door that would take us into the Fast Fare Pump and Shop.

Once she joined me, I held my hand out to her. She took it and smiled at me. All of a sudden, she seemed to be the youngest not me.

I stepped in and opened my mouth in shock. Sitting at the counter was Big Red and Grace. Both had aged about twenty-five years but not so much that I didn't know them immediately.

"What took you so long?" Big Red asked before I could introduce Chris and myself. He stood, walked towards me with his big hand extended.

"We were gonna go home an hour ago but didn't dare. We were afraid we'd miss you." Grace said.

"I stopped to get my sister." I said. "This is Chris. I hope that was alright."

"We were counting on you to bring her." Grace said coming around and hugging us both. Chris hugged her back then looked back at me. She was going to love it here.

"Mat...um Matty...who are these people. How do you know them? How did they know we were coming? You said you didn't know where you were going." She half whispered half spoke out loud.

"Grandma must have told them." I said then realized that didn't help her much.

"She did." Big Red said.

"How long have you two been married?" I asked, remembering how Big Red felt about Grace twenty five years ago.

"Did everyone know how you felt about me except me?" Grace asked blushing.

"You had a lot on your mind." I said. At that, they looked at each other.

"Yes I suppose I did."

The conversation was weird for Chris. She only knew one of the players. That made it weirder. Chris squeezed my hand. She was nervous and she was uncomfortable. She wanted to go so she started pulling me towards the door.

"It's a long story Chris." Big Red said. "Why don't we get the two of you settled in and we'll do our best to explain." At that, he opened the door. "As for the answer to your question Matty, Grace and I just celebrated twenty of the best years of our lives."

"Congratulations!" Chris and I said together.

"Thanks." They both smiled at each other.

"Got a job lined up for you at the library." Grace said to Chris. "You can start whenever you're ready.

"What?" Chris asked. She was totally shocked. So was I. How could they have known of Chris' desire to be a Librarian? "Are you kidding? I love books." Chris said then stopped and looked at Grace, Big Red then me.

"Don't look at me. I didn't tell them. Truth be known Chris, I'd forgotten." This time I dropped my head feeling ashamed. She squeezed my hand again.

"Well I never forgot what you wanted to do." Chris said smiling at me. "You always wanted to be a vet."

"And a vet you shall be. That's why you have to start sooner rather than later Matty. Sidney would like to train you so that you can take over. He wants to retire."

"Sidney?" Chris asked.

"Yeah. He's the local vet." Chris took a deep breath and looked at me.

"Being a vet was all Matty talked about when we were kids. Well, that's all he talked about before our dad died." She added. "When you're telling me how you knew we were coming and who we were, will you also tell me how you knew what our hearts desires were?"

"We'll do our best." Grace said putting her arm around her and squeezing her tight." I could tell Chris enjoyed being hugged. Her eyes were shining like they did when she came down on Christmas morning. Before our father died.

"Grandma." I said looking at Big Red. He and Grace looked at each other then they looked at me. "When do I get to see her?"

"Matty, honey, I thought you understood." Grace said putting one arm around me.

"I don't understand anything. Except that I met a nice old lady who looked past my wall of hate and self pity, found a heart in there and touched it. I want to tell her thank you."

"You just did Matty." Grace said pulling me close to her. "You see honey, Grandma has been dead for ten years."